IT WAS ALWAYS US 2

Love In These Miami Streets

ANGIE HAYES

This book is about strength and determination, so it is solely dedicated to my great nephew; DeQuan Marquel West Jr (Dj).
Dj, you are the epitome of a true little fighter, and you're my hero. Every day I pray for your strength and thank God for allowing you to still be here with us. TT loves you nugget. Today, tomorrow and always.

OTHER BOOKS BY ANGIE HAYES

From Mistress To Wife

PREVIOUSLY IN, IT WAS ALWAYS US: LOVE IN THESE MIAMI STREETS

SKY

I was in my truck, heading to T.G.I. Friday's to meet Isis. My ribs were still sore, but I tried my best to block out the pain. Besides, I wanted to get out of the house and see what it was that Isis had to say. When I woke up this morning, Ronnie had left me a note saying that he dropped Imani off to daycare and was out handling business. I didn't even bother to let him know that I was heading out to meet with my sister. He was already overprotective enough lately.

As I drove, my mind went back to Katrice. I really missed my friend. We had never had a fallen out before this, and it was killing me not to talk to her. Deep down, I knew that she didn't mean any ill will, but right now, I just couldn't be so open to forgiving her. I don't give a fuck what she thought; she still should have never kept those things from me about Damon. Had I known then, I wouldn't be going through this now.

Before I knew it, I was pulling into the restaurant's parking lot. I sent Isis a text letting her know that I was there, and she replied that she was already inside, towards the back waiting. I climbed out of my truck and walked outside. Heading towards the back, I spotted Isis sitting at a booth, texting on her phone. She looked up as she saw me approaching the booth.

"What's up, Isis?" I greeted her as I slid into the seat across from her in the booth.

"Hey, Sky, thanks for coming," she responded.

"I was shocked that you called me because we never saw eye to eye," I reminded her.

"I know, and that's why I wanted to meet with you, to tell you how sorry I am. I know the shit Momma was doing to you was wrong, yet I never defended you. I also knew that I was treating you unfairly as well, so for everything, I truly apologize, Sky."

I couldn't tell if what she was saying was sincere or not because I never heard her apologize for shit before, especially to me.

"I appreciate your apology," I replied with a faint smile.

My gut was telling me that she was still full of shit, which is why I didn't tell her that I accepted her apology... I only appreciated it. I refused to be blindsided by a snake bitch again.

"No problem, are you ready to order?" she asked, grabbing the menu and starting to look it over.

I picked mine up and looked at it as well. Shortly after, the waitress came over and took our drink and food orders.

"So, what happened to your face?" Isis asked, looking at me from across the table once the waitress left.

My bruises weren't that visible if you were far away from me, but up close, you could see them through my makeup, and I still had the bandage over my nose.

"I got in a car accident and hit my head on the steering wheel," I lied. There was no way in hell I was about to tell her the truth.

"Damn, that's fucked up," she said, short, as she pulled her phone back out of her purse and started texting on it.

This bitch didn't even ask if I was okay or if Imani was in the accident with me! If I had not already ordered my food and drinks, I would leave right fucking now. I honestly felt there was no reason for me to be here at all. The waitress came back with our drinks and appetizers.

"So, how are the kids? I miss them." I was trying to make light conversation so that the time could go by quickly.

"Girl, still bad as hell. You can come get their asses anytime you want!" Isis laughed, but I knew she was dead ass serious.

She never wanted to be around her kids and always tried to push them off on other folks every chance she got. Isis didn't give a fuck if she had just met you that day; she'll still let her kids spend the night at your house and won't even call to check on them. Between her and my no-good ass momma, who also just let them run around and do what the fuck they wanted, I was the only stability they had.

"I'll get them soon so that they can spend time with Imani," I told her.

"Where you staying at now anyway?" she questioned.

"With a friend," I replied, not telling her more.

Right then, the waitress came out with our food and both of us dug in. The conversation was light and pretty much nonexistent. It seemed like every other minute, Isis kept checking her phone and texting on it. When we were finished eating, I offered to pay the tab, and Isis quickly accepted, just like I thought she would. You would think that since she was the one that invited me out to lunch, she would pay.

"I'm glad you decided to have lunch with me," she said to me when we walked outside.

"No problem; thanks for inviting me," I said as I took my keys out of my purse, getting ready to head to my truck.

Her phone went off again. "Damn," she said out loud.

"What's wrong?" I asked.

"I caught a ride here because my car has been acting up. The person who was supposed to pick me back up just texted me and said that they were gonna be an hour late because they got tied up with something. You think you could drop me off at their house instead, so I won't have to wait out here for no damn hour?" Isis asked me.

"Where do they stay?" I asked her, not really wanting to take her in the first place.

"Right here in Pembroke, by the mall."

I agreed to drop her off since it was on my way back to Weston to Ronnie's house. We walked to my car and got inside.

"Damn sis, I see you came up. I thought you said that you were in a car accident?" Isis said to me as she looked around my truck as I pulled out the parking lot.

Ronnie ended up buying me a Mercedes G-Wagon that same week I got home from the hospital. I just laughed lightly at Isis' comment.

"I was, but I wasn't the one driving. So, what's the exact address so I can put it in my GPS?" I asked, not wanting to tell her my fucking *business and wanting to drop her ass off wherever it was she needed to go.*

"Uh, I don't know his exact address, but I do know the way there. Make a left here," Isis instructed.

I followed her directions as she went back to texting on her phone. Minutes later, she looked up.

"It's gonna be traffic going this way; make a right at this light and let's take the back roads," Isis suggested.

Soon as I got to the light, I made a right like she told me to and started driving down the back road. We were driving for a good ten minutes when I heard a loud bang and my truck swerved off the road, into this ditch, and hit a tree. My airbag released and opened in my face, which caused me to yell out in pain.

"Oh my God!" I moaned out loud, coughing up blood from my mouth. I was sure that my lip was busted again and my nose, which still wasn't fully healed, was throbbing with pain.

I looked over to my right to make sure that Isis was alright, but all I saw was my passenger door opened and her nowhere in sight. My head was pounding from the impact of my truck hitting the tree and the airbag exploding in my face. I slowly unbuckled my seatbelt and looked around to see where my phone had fallen so that I could call for help.

"Looking for this?" I heard a deep voice from behind me.

I turned back around and came face to face with a person that I never thought that I would ever lay eyes on again.

"Gerald?" I blurted out.

"That's right, and since I'm here, you won't be needing this." He was holding up my phone and then slid it in his back pocket.

With the pain that I was in, I knew there was no way that I could run from him. I was beyond terrified and didn't know what to expect next.

"We are in for an overdue conversation, Sky." Gerald grinned as he came closer to me in the truck.

Before I could try to say anything else, he put a rag over my already bruised nose and held it there. I was struggling and crying, trying to remove his hand because I was in unbearable pain. Suddenly, it felt like everything became heavy and then I stopped moving all together and fell limp.

RONNIE

"Man, what is this about!" Damon screamed, tied up to the chair.

His face was bloody and one of his eyes was closed shut. My boys did a job on this nigga, which was a sight to see for me.

"Oh, you don't know why you're here?" I asked, calmly, as I pulled up a chair to sit across from him.

I cleared the room of everyone, but Nick and I. Soon as Damon came through, thinking he was about to re-up, I had my boys snatch his ass up and bring him into the isolated back room.

"No! You told me to come and do a pickup! Next thing I know, I'm getting my ass beat and tied up to a chair!" Damon yelled, spitting out blood.

No matter how loud this pussy yelled, nobody was going to hear him. I had this room padded and soundproof.

"So you thought that after you had done that shit you did to Sky, I was gone let that ride?" I questioned, looking at his ass in his face.

He became tense and just stared at me.

"What's wrong, fuck boy? Can't say shit now?" Nick asked, standing behind me.

"I ain't do shit to Sky! If anything, I was good to her and Imani when yo' ass wasn't around!" Damon yelled, looking at me.

I stood up and knocked him in his shit, causing him to fall over in the chair and hit the floor. I picked him back up and sat him upright.

"Don't you ever in your life speak my family's name again!" I got in his face, jacking him up by his bloody shirt. "And I'mma make sure you don't; Nick, hand me the case," I said, reaching my arm behind me as I kept staring at this fuck boy.

Nick put the small case in my hand, and I brought it around to the front of me. I opened it up and took out the pliers. I also took the gloves off and began to put them on. Nick came up behind Damon and grabbed his back, holding it in a tight grip. Damon started trying to scream and squirm in the chair; that's when I punched his ass in the stomach to shut him up. Right when I was about to reach for his tongue and cut that shit, my phone started vibrating in my pocket. I know I should have ignored it and finished this nigga instead, but he wasn't going anywhere anytime soon. I pulled it out of my pocket and saw Sky's name on my display.

"Hold this motherfucker right quick," I said as I reached for my phone in my pocket.

I walked away from where Damon was being held so that Sky couldn't hear his bitch ass.

"What's up, baby, you okay?" I answered the phone.

"Nah, she ain't okay, fuck nigga, but I'm about to take really good care of her," I heard a male voice on the other end of the phone.

I took the phone from my ear, looking at it to make sure that that was Sky's number calling me.

"Who the fuck is this?" I yelled, putting the phone back to my ear.

"The motherfucker who got yo' bitch, and if you wanna see her again, I want two million dollars by tomorrow night. If not, after I finish fucking the shit out this good ass pussy, I'mma put a bullet in this bitch head. Once I'm done with Sky, then I'm coming for little Imani." He laughed into the phone.

My palms became sweaty and my heart was racing. I was so fucking mad all I saw was red!

"Nigga, it's obvious you don't know who I am," I said in a low, menacing tone.

"I know exactly who you are, Ronald Johnson!" he called my government name. "If you think I'm bullshitting, try me! I'll call you in the morning to let you know the details on the drop." Then, he hung up before I could say anything else.

My phone vibrated again; this time, it was a picture message coming through. I opened it and saw what looked to be Sky, tied up with a blindfold on, laying on a dirty ass mattress on the floor.

"Fuck!" I screamed as I ran back into the room where Nick and Damon were.

"What's going on?" Nick asked me as I went charging towards Damon.

"Some motherfucker just called my phone from Sky's phone, telling me that he got her. Then, he sent me this pic!" I yelled out, showing Nick my phone.

"What the fuck!" He snatched it from my hand and stared at.

My adrenalin was pumping, and I was about to body some-fuck-ing-body right now!

"Where the fuck she at, bitch boy!" I yelled, getting up in Damon's face. I pulled my Glock from my waist and pointed it at Damon's head.

"I don't know what you talking about. I swear!" he stuttered.

At this point, it didn't even matter if he did or not!

"I don't give a fuck if you're my brother or not. Niggas that fuck with my bitch, I put they ass in a special place until I get there!"

"Brother?" Damon said, confused.

Before he could open his mouth again, I let two off to his head.

Sometimes I wonder if love is enough

Chapter One

SKY

I woke up groggy, with the smell of strong piss hitting my nostrils! Trying to move, I noticed that my hands were tied behind my back and I was lying down on a lumpy ass mattress on the floor. Looking around, I took notice that I was in a small ass room with one window boarded up, a chair sitting in the middle of the floor, and this disgusting ass mattress I was laying on against a wall. I struggled to sit up and push myself up against the wall, when suddenly, the sound of the locks on the door being unlocked from the outside stopped me in fear, letting me know that someone was coming.

In walked Gerald's ugly ass with this stupid ass grin on his face. Lord knows I was terrified because I didn't know what this nigga was about to do to me. So, I just sat up as much as I could and pressed myself against the wall, staring at him as he walked towards me.

"You finally awake." Gerald said to me as he came and stood on the side of the mattress.

Not saying anything, I just continued to stare at him.

"I see you trying to be hard and not say shit, but I bet if I stuck my dick in yo' mouth, you'd open that motherfucker then." he laughed.

"What do you want and where the fuck is my sister?" I finally spoke out.

I still hadn't seen any sign of Isis since my truck was run off the road, and became worried that this sick fuck might have done something to her.

"Fuck you worried about her ass for? What you need to be worried about is if I'm gonna let yo' ass out of here alive and raise our precious little daughter, Imani, on my own." Gerald replied smirking.

My heart instantly started beating fast and sweat began to pour down my face at what he had just said. How the fuck did he even know about Imani, let alone her name? At this point, my mind was already made up to do whatever it took to get the fuck out of here and make it to my daughter before Gerald could lay a fucking finger on her.

"Gerald, I don't know what you're talking about, because we don't have a daughter together." I said to him with a straight face.

He walked over to me and slapped the shit out of me. My body fell over onto the mattress from the impact. I sat back up against the wall, breathing heavy with tears forming in the corner of my eyes.

"Bitch, keep lying and the next time I'mma put yo' head right through the fucking wall!" Gerald threatened. "So, let's try this again. Why didn't you tell me I had a daughter?"

"She i-isn't y-yours." I stuttered, trembling from so much fear.

"Really, because her age and the timeline of when you gave me that sweet ass pussy—"

"I didn't give you anything, you raped me!" I blurted out, interrupting him in mid-sentence.

"Raped you? Bitch, please. You thought your pussy was too good for a nigga like me since you started fucking with Ronnie's ass. Matter of fact, your ass thought you were better than everybody else. Thinking that you were top notch shit when you got with that nigga, but quickly forgot how you and those other lil hoes you were hanging with were fucking and sucking niggas off for cash." Gerald laughed.

Being reminded of my past was something I wasn't trying to get into with him. All I wanted to do was make it out of here alive, get to Imani, and get as far away from Miami as I could.

"Look, I did as you asked. I didn't tell anyone what you had done to me, and I even moved away from the apartments. Why won't you just leave me alone and let me live my life?" I pleaded, now crying.

"Because I had yo' ass first and then you just up and stop fucking with me because a motherfucker with heavier pockets came along!" he yelled, coming closer to the edge of the bed again.

"Gerald, we were never together. We only had that one encounter in your car that night and that was it!" I yelled back, hoping that he could get the shit through his fucking head.

He stood there for a moment, staring at me until he spoke. "You know what, you just like the rest of these dumb ass hoes out here. Go around teasing muthafuckas and advertising ya pussy, then when a nigga tries to get at you, you wanna scream rape."

I couldn't believe the shit that had just come out of Gerald's mouth. It was as if he actually believed that I had sex with him willingly! Never mind the fact that he held a gun to me and threatened to kill me and my granny if I had told anyone what he had done. I guess that's not considered rape in this sick fuck's book!

"You know I was feeling you, Sky; I always have. Now, the thought of us having a child together makes this shit more complete for me. I stayed in the background and handled shit for us just to make sure we could be together with no problems."

"What do you mean stayed in the background and handled shit for us?" I asked Gerald, confused.

"How you think Ronnie got knocked off with those drugs in his truck? I was the one that made that shit happen." he laughed.

"So, you're the one that set him up?"

"I'm not gone repeat myself. You heard what I just said; I handled it. If it weren't for the fucked-up system, his ass would still be in that motherfucker and you'd be with me with no problems. So, check this out, I already hit up Ronnie and told him that I had you and wanted two million dollars for your head. His ass will do anything for you, so I'm expecting him to make a drop with the cash sometime tomorrow when I call him back with the time and place. Once I get the money, you can forget about that nigga altogether. You and Imani coming with me and getting the fuck out of Florida." Gerald stated.

I swear this dude was certified crazy! Not only was he the one that set Ronnie up to go to jail, but he honestly thought that I was going to go away and be with him!

"I don't know what the fuck you got going on in that fucked up head of yours, but whether I was with Ronnie or not, I would never be with your sorry, crazy ass!" I blurted out.

Gerald just stood there with a calm look on his face, then suddenly, it turned to rage. He charged at me on the bed and punched me in my face, which caused me to be in a daze.

"Stupid ass bitch! I'mma show you what's gone happen every time you come out the mouth slick to me!"

Gerald pulled me farther down on the bed, turned me over on my stomach, and yanked down my shorts and panties altogether.

"Gerald, please don't do this!" I pleaded, in fear of knowing what was about to happen.

"Nah, you were just talking big shit, talking about you wouldn't be with me! Well, I'm about to show yo' ass just who run this muthafucka!"

On my stomach, with my hands still tied behind my back and nowhere for me to go, I started kicking and screaming in hopes that someone would hear me.

"Shut yo' ass up because ain't nobody gone hear shit!" Gerald choked me from behind. "Now, the more you keep moving, the harder you're gonna make this shit!"

Gerald straddled my legs, as I felt him spread my ass cheeks apart.

"Since I already know how good this pussy is, let me see what this ass working with." I heard him say.

I tried squirming more, but his body weight was too heavy for me to move. I felt Gerald dick head pressing its way into the opening of my asshole. Screaming, this time in excruciating pain as his dick tore into my asshole. My insides were on fire as my ass felt like it was tearing more and more with each thrust from Gerald penetrating me. I never had anal sex and never wanted to for this exact reason right here—pain! I stopped screaming and just laid there numb as Gerald continued to fuck me in my ass. I closed my eyes and tried to focus on Ronnie and Imani, hoping that I could make it out of here and see them again because right now, I felt like my soul had left my body.

Chapter Two

RONNIE

"*A*h fuck!" Damon screamed out.

"Shut yo' bitch ass up! You lucky I didn't light yo' chest up!" I yelled as I slapped Damon across his mouth with the butt of my gun.

His ass fell to the floor again, tied up to the chair, screaming like a lil bitch. After I had received that fucked up phone call earlier telling me that they got Sky, I shot Damon's ass once in the leg and once in the shoulder purposely. Although I wanted to dead this nigga, I still didn't know if he had anything to do with Sky being kidnapped.

I went over to Damon and bent down to pick his ass back up in the chair. Nick was over in the corner on his phone.

"I'mma ask yo' ass one more time, then this time, if you lie to me, I'm putting one in between yo muthafuckin' eyes and then make a visit over to ya momma's crib. Where the fuck is Sky?" I yelled in his face, pointing my gun at his temple.

"I promise you man; I don't know shit about where Sky is!" his bitch ass cried out spitting blood out of his mouth.

I stared him dead in his face and saw that this muthafucka was nothing but straight pussy! If he didn't have anything to do with my baby being taken, then I was about to tear these Miami streets up!

"Aye, Ronnie, you said whoever called you called you from Sky's phone, right?" Nick interrupted, coming up from behind me.

"Yeah, why?" I asked as I turned my attention to him.

"Sis got an iPhone, right?" he asked.

"Yeah" I answered him again.

"Turn on your "Find My iPhone app" and see if you can pick up her location that way. If those muthafuckas dumb as we think they are, we'll be able to find them that way. In the meantime, I got my boy pulling her phone records now to see which tower and location the call was made from." Nick let me know.

I took my phone back out of my pocket and turned on the app as instructed, and put in Sky's number. The phone was in search mode, then I finally got a message saying 'phone not found'. I tried it again, only to get the same message.

"Fuck man!" I screamed out.

"What's up, no luck?" Nick came back over and asked me.

"Naw, man. Whoever has her phone must have disabled her shit." I told him.

Turning back around to face Damon, I shot that nigga in his other arm and kicked his ass over again in his chair knocking him back to the floor.

"I know you pissed Ronnie—shit, so am I—but you have to keep a cool head if we gone find lil sis." Nick reminded me.

I closed my eyes and took a couple of deep breaths, trying to calm myself down. He was right; I needed to have a clear mind and not react off the adrenalin I had pumping through me right now.

"You right bruh. Did we get the location from the towers yet?"

"My boy said give him a minute; he'll be calling me right back with some information. In the meantime, tell me what was said again from whomever it was that called from Sky phone." Nick asked me.

"Basically that he has Sky and that he wanted me to make a drop of two million, and that he would call back with a time and place." I relayed the message again to Nick. "You already know the money ain't shit, but it's the fact that whoever this is seems to think that me and my family is something to play with is what's gone get these muthafuckas bodies floating in the Everglades. You already know I'll do an L for Sky and Imani!" I seethed, punching the padded wall.

"Did you recognize the voice on the other end?" Nick questioned.

"Naw, they were using a voice changer so that I wouldn't recognize it, which is letting me know that it must be somebody I know; and I have a feeling who the fuck that might be." I replied.

"Gerald's fuck ass." Nick responded nodding his head up and down in agreement.

"You already know. That pussy been trying to snake me since he called himself trying to set me up with putting those drugs in my car." I explained.

"I told you that we should have handled his ass when you first jumped ship from jail. Now, you believe that fuck nigga when he said he didn't know anything about Sky being taken?" Nick asked me, pointing at Damon who was still on the floor, laying there groaning and bleeding.

"I don't know, but at this point, it doesn't even matter because his ass is just as dead now anyway." I said as I walked over to where Damon was lying and kicked him in his stomach.

I didn't give a fuck if he was my half-brother or not. In my eyes, he was just as much the cause of Sky being gone right now as the muthafucka who had her. When I first asked my source, Rob, for information on Damon, the last thing I expected was to find out that me, him, and Katrice had the same daddy; especially since my uncle never mentioned anything about my daddy having any outside family.

Seems like not only had he become a dope head, but he was also a fucking rolling stone. He had a whole other family out here with Damon, Katrice, and their momma. Apparently, my momma found out about it and confronted their momma, but my old boy never stopped seeing her. But not only did I find out that he's my brother, but that his bitch ass was also married with a daughter.

I sat Damon back up in his chair as he groaned out in pain. I stood back and looked at how fucked up he was. "Look bitch ass nigga, if you don't open yo' mouth and tell me what the fuck I need to know, I'mma finish yo' punk ass off!"

"I promise you, Ronnie, I don't have shit to do with what's going on with Sky. I love her ass just like you do." he stuttered, coughing up blood.

"Love her? Fuck nigga, you beat her like she was a nigga in the streets, raped her like the punk ass bitch you are, and let's not forget how you got a fucking wife and kid that I'm sure Sky knew nothing about. That ain't love! You ain't shit but a coward pussy who's about to piss me off even more!" I yelled getting up in his face.

Damon stared at me with one eye while the other was closed shut, and then put his head down. I heard Nick on the phone behind me, sounding like he was getting confirmation on something.

"Aight, we got a location; the call came from a tower from Overtown. Also, one of Gerald's workers just confirmed that he has a duck off spot there as well. He said went over there one time to do a pick up from him. Seems like that's the house where he also keeps his guns he's selling, so that confirms that he's the one behind this. I got the address and we already loaded; what you wanna do next?" Nick asked me, as he stood there looking at me waiting for the next move.

Suddenly, my phone rang. I looked at it and saw that it was Sky's number.

"I'm getting a call from Sky's phone again." I informed Nick as I answered it.

"Yeah" I answered the phone.

"Change of plans. I want you to meet me tonight at Key Biscayne Bridge. Put the money in a red book bag." the caller said, disguising their voice again, but I was pretty sure it was this fuck nigga Gerald.

"I ain't doing shit until I know Sky is alive first." I said into the phone.

"Take the bass out yo' voice, homeboy! I'm the one calling the fucking shots, but I'll let you hear yo' bitch's voice one last time." I heard him tell Sky to open her fucking mouth and say something into the phone.

"Ronnie" she cried out.

I closed my eyes and sighed in relief, knowing that she was still alive.

"I'm here baby. I got you, don't worry." I said low into the phone.

"Alright, you heard her ass, now meet me on the bridge at eleven tonight. Soon as you hand me the bag, I'll give you yo' bitch back. Besides, I've been having enough fun with her pussy and sweet ass for one day." He laughed into the phone. "Oh, I already know you don't deal with the police, so I don't have to worry about you involving them, but if you try any other slick shit, I'll blow this bitch's brains out and throw her ass in the river. I got eyes on you, so try me." The call disconnected.

"He said he wants me to meet him on Key Biscayne Bridge at eleven tonight with all the money in a red book bag." I said, looking over at Nick.

"Fuck he think, we in some type of movie or some shit?" Nick blurted out pissed.

"I don't give a fuck what he thinks, all I know is that we about to load up and go to his ass sooner than he expects. As for him," I said, turning my attention back to Damon. "You a straight pussy who's about to be fucked. I wasn't gone kill yo' ass, but I changed my mind." I raised my gun and shot Damon clean between his eyes. Soon as his body fell over, I stood over him and emptied two more into his chest; this time, hitting his ass there.

"Tell the boys to load up. That worker for Gerald, bring his ass along too. Call the clean-up crew to clean this mutha-fucka up, and let everyone know that I'll be the one handling Gerald personally and that if a hair is touched on Sky, I'm bodying their asses too."

Once everybody was in place, we all rolled out, ready for war.

Chapter Three

GERALD

I had just finished fucking Sky for the third time since I brought her here to my little duck off spot no one knew about. I hated that she brought me to do this to her, because the truth of the matter is, I was obsessed with her ass. I have always been attracted to Sky, watching her from the background every day when she used to hang out with those other hoes, and I was happy as hell the day she agreed to let me eat her pussy that night in my car. I thought after that, she would let me fuck her on the regular and eventually have feelings for me too, but that wasn't the case.

Next thing I knew, I looked up and she was with Ronnie. Ronnie, now that was a muthafucka I couldn't wait to put six feet deep. I couldn't stand his cocky ass since the first day I approached him for work. He looked his nose down at me as if I was coming to him for a fucking handout. After slanging for him for about six months, he saw how hard my feet were hitting the streets and gave me my own corner and team. I was making a little more cash, but nowhere near what Ronnie was making, of course.

That's when I started my side hustle of selling guns. I got the hookup with these Haitian cats from Lil Haiti. They were way on the other side of town, so I didn't have to worry about Ronnie or anyone else finding out about shit that I had going on. Anyway, I figured the more money I made, Sky would see me as a nigga that could take care of her just as well as Ronnie and be with me, but that shit proved to be bullshit too.

More and more, those two started kicking it heavy. She even stopped hanging around those other lil hoes she used to run with and became straight and narrow with going to school everyday and shit. Soon, word on the streets was that Sky was off limits. That's when I decided to set Ronnie's ass up by putting drugs in his truck and calling the police to tip them off. I went by the spot to do a pick-up and saw that he was there. Soon as I collected my stash, I walked outside and noticed that no one was out there and that his truck was parked in the cut, out of view.

Suddenly, the idea of putting my stash in his shit came to mind. It was just my luck that his truck was unlocked. I guess he knew that muthafuckas around here knew not to fuck with his shit, which was true. I quietly opened his back door, and slipped the drugs in the backseat behind the passenger seat and got out of dodge without being noticed.

I stayed low-key the rest of the day and followed him, up

until nightfall, and that's when I called the cops and gave them a tip, along with his license plate. Hearing that he got knocked off was music to my ears; I was sure Sky's ass would come to her senses then. Instead, she called herself still trying to hold that nigga down while he was locked up and not giving me or anyone else any play.

That night when I saw her at the apartments at the party, she looked good as fuck! I couldn't contain myself. That's when I tried to approach her and just talk to her at first, but she gave me a funky ass attitude and that's when I snapped. I honestly didn't mean to take it there with Sky, but I was tired of her treating me as if I was a fuck nigga in the streets.

Although I threatened to kill her and her grandma if she told anyone that I had raped her, I didn't mean it. Just like now, when I told Ronnie that I would kill her if he tried some slick shit when he brought me the cash. The only promise I plan to make good on was killing his ass. I walked out of the room, leaving Sky lying there, just staring at the wall as I went to get a rag and soap to clean her up.

By me fucking her in her ass, she had blood and feces all over the mattress and the room began to stink. I went to the bathroom and grabbed the washrag, a small bucket from underneath the sink, and filled it with hot water. I walked back into the room where Sky was still laying like she was lifeless and began to wipe her off. She tried scooting away from me, even though her hands were still tied behind her back, and moaned out in pain when I touched her.

"If you stay still, you wouldn't be in pain and I could get you cleaned up." I told her as I snatched her closer to me.

"I don't understand why you still try to fight me Sky. Don't you see how much I care about yo' ass?" I said as I washing her up.

"Please let me go Gerald. I promise you I won't say anything." she cried softly.

"Didn't I tell yo' ass that me, you, and Imani were leaving Florida together? Ain't no letting you go!" I yelled at her ass, getting pissed off. "I don't know what it's going to take for you to get it through your fucking thick head; you my bitch now!" I nudged her forehead.

Sky just continued to lay there, crying silently as I finished cleaning her up. Once I was done, I left back out the room and went into the kitchen to get her something to drink. I grabbed a bottle of water out of the fridge and went back into the room where Sky was.

"Here, drink this." I said to her as I opened the water and put it to her mouth.

At first, she was hesitant, but eventually, she took a swallow from the bottle while staring at me.

"Good, you hungry?" I asked. She nodded her head up and down, saying yes.

"Aight, I'll be back with something to eat." I got back up and left out of the room again.

I hope now Sky realizes that shit can go a lot smoother once her ass gets on board.

Chapter Four

SKY

I was in so much pain that my ass felt like it was on fire. This was the worst violation that I could have possibly endured! Gerald had taken all my dignity and self-respect and it didn't take much for him to do. At least I now know the motive behind the fucked-up shit that had happened to me these past two and a half years of my life, and Gerald was responsible for much of it.

I couldn't believe how obsessed this muthafucka was with being with me and the hate he had for Ronnie. *Lord, please just let me make it out of here alive and to see my baby again.* I prayed silently as I closed my eyes and began to cry again. If it weren't for Imani, I would pray that he just let this crazy fuck kill me and get this shit over with instead.

I felt like the most disgusting individual still laying here on this dirty ass mattress, tied up, and naked from the waist down, exposed with what I assumed was blood still sliding out of my ass from the tearing. Although Gerald called himself cleaning me up and giving me something to drink, that still didn't excuse the fact that he raped me again; this time, more than once.

At this point, I didn't know what was going to happen to me. I didn't know if I would see Imani again or if Isis was alive. The tiny comfort of hope I had was when Gerald told me that he had already contacted Ronnie and told him that he wanted two million from him in order to get me back, and that they would meet up to get the money. That gave me faith in knowing that Ronnie would do whatever it took to get me back. I was just worried that he wouldn't catch on to the extra shit Gerald had planned before it was too late.

While Gerald was out of the room, getting me something to eat as he claimed, I took this time to myself and closed my eyes. I wanted to go to sleep and wake up lying in bed with Ronnie and Imani laying in between us, hoping this would have all been a bad dream. I must have dozed off because I jumped out of my sleep to the sound of loud popping sounds.

Panic and fear set in when I realized that it was the sound of guns blazing through the house. Scared and not able to move that much, I scooted myself closer to the wall, balled up in a fetal position, and closed my eyes tight. Shaking and not knowing what the fuck was going on out there, or if a bullet was about to hit me, I pissed on myself all over the mattress.

Minutes later, I heard the door of the room being kicked in. Staying on my side with my eyes still closed tight, I heard voices in the room but was still too afraid to turn around and see where they were coming from.

"I found her, she's in here!" I heard someone yell out.

I just knew shit was all over for me now. Here I was, eighteen, and about to leave my baby alone in this fucked up ass world without a momma. I heard the footsteps get closer to me and I was scared stiff. Then suddenly, I felt someone put something over me and lifted me in their arms.

"I got you, baby, I'm here." I heard Ronnie say.

I screamed out, crying as he carried me out.

Chapter Five

RONNIE

HREE MONTHS LATER...

"Sky listen, I need you to get up and get yo' shit together so we can go meet with my lawyer and get Imani back! I'm sick of this shit with you man!" I screamed as Sky laid in the bed with her back facing me as she stared out the window.

I walked over to her side of the bed and yanked the covers off her. Instead of getting a reaction out of her like I hoped, she still just laid there, staring out the window, not moving a fucking inch.

"So you just gone keep ignoring me like I'm not standing here Sky?" I asked, but she still wasn't saying shit.

"Come on baby, let's go downstairs for a minute. I made some fresh tea." I heard Ms. Mary say. I looked up to see her standing in the bedroom doorway.

I stared down at Sky for a couple more seconds before taking Ms. Mary up on her offer and leaving out the room. I slammed the door shut behind me, frustrated. I stormed down the stairs and went into the kitchen and sat down at the island. Ms. Mary came right behind me and went over to the cabinets and grabbed two cups from out of there. She went over to the stove and poured hot water into the cups and put the tea bags in there.

"You have to give her time, baby." Ms. Mary said as she placed my cup in front of me and took a seat next to me.

"Time? Ms. Mary, it's been three months and it's still the same shit with her. Excuse my language." I apologized when I saw her giving me a stern look.

"I know, and I know it's frustrating, but right now, she's in a dark place where only the good Lord can help her out of, but He can't do it alone. She needs to find a way to help herself so that He can help her. Faith without work is dead." Ms. Mary said, trying to add as much comfort as she could to the situation.

The day I finally brought Sky home safely from when she was kidnapped, I opted out of taking her back to the hospital and called Ms. Mary instead to come and look after her. She was bruised so badly and had been raped once again; this time, in the anal area. She was too traumatized to go back to the hospital and be questioned all over again, especially since she was recently there from what Damon had done to her.

So, I called Ms. Mary and she's been here ever since. She

even decided to take a leave of absence from her job and stay here with us until things got better with Sky and Imani, but it hadn't. Sky was still in a state of deep depression and Imani was now in the custody of Sky's momma, Evelyn.

That's right, Evelyn's fat, trifling ass ended up getting temporary custody of Imani from the courts, and I blamed myself for that. When everything was taking place with the whole Gerald situation, Sky was left in daycare way longer than her pick up time and the school contacted Evelyn to pick her up since they couldn't get in contact with Sky. I knew I should have called Katrice to go and pick her up, but my mind at the time was only on getting Sky back.

Evelyn took that as an opportunity to run her fat ass down to the courts and file for temporary custody of Imani, claiming abandonment. With Sky not fighting her or contesting it, the courts agreed. Evelyn filed with the courts saying that Sky was incompetent and unable to properly care for Imani. Not willing to let her ass just take Imani away, I immediately petitioned the courts for a DNA test to prove that Imani was mine, which turned out to be true, and that I could gain custody of her while Sky got help.

Ever since Evelyn got Imani, she hadn't allowed me or Sky to visit her; not that Sky was trying to anyway. Everyone knew the only reason that bitch wanted Imani in the first place was so that she could continue to get benefits from the system.

I know Sky was fucked up about all the shit she had been through, but I would have at least thought that getting her daughter back would be enough motivation to pull her out of this depression.

"So, what did your lawyer say the next step would be?" Ms. Mary asked, taking a sip of her tea.

"Now we're just waiting for a court hearing. He filed a motion and petitioned the court for an emergency hearing, but since it's dealing with a custody hearing, things take time with the family court. In the meantime, you know I already severed ties with my old lifestyle and have been cleaning up my money so that I won't have a problem showing the courts that I am the better fit for my baby girl." I explained to Ms. Mary.

It was partially true. After handling Damon and Gerald, I did bow out of the dope game. I couldn't risk the fact that muthafuckas would still try to come for my family, and seeing how much my lifestyle was affecting Sky, it was easy to choose her and Imani over everything else. Nick decided that it was time for him to leave the game as well and followed suit.

We made a vow when we first started this, that since we got in this together, that we would leave out this bitch together and that's exactly what we had done. We both had more than enough money to live on and investments to make and cash in on. So, we turned everything over to our boy, Rob. He had the smarts and the street cred to handle everything. He had also been around us long enough to know how shit operated. I was still in the background though, watching and helping him from time to time, but that was just until he didn't need me anymore.

It took some convincing to get my connect to start dealing with Rob instead of me, but eventually, he agreed. Since I never fucked him over and neither had my uncle when he was alive and dealing with him, he left the option for me to return to him if I ever decided to come back into the game. I had no plans on doing that though. My face was still clean in these streets, my name still rang bells, and my money was long.

All I wanted to do was settle down and make sure Sky was fulfilling her dreams by going to college and me being a family man, taking care of my woman and child.

"Well, I'm glad you finally decided to leave that mess you were dealing with alone. Living that way is only temporary, so you were blessed child, to make it out in one peace. Now, as far as Sky goes, she's gonna come around. It's just gonna take some mean pushing, that's all." Ms. Mary assured me.

"But what else can I do to push her? I tried everything I could think of. I've been giving her space. I had a psychiatrist come to the house and try to talk to her, I had Katrice coming back around to try and get her to get out of this funk, and even called her momma and begged her to just let me get Imani so that she could see her, but nothing has worked. I'm starting to feel less of a man that I can't help my woman Ms. Mary."

"Believe me when I say, you are far from less of a man. Everything you did and are still doing is what a real man does. Now, you just need to focus on getting nana's baby back home and I'll continue to work on Ms. Sky." Ms. Mary rubbed me on my shoulder as she got up and left out the kitchen.

Chapter Six

KATRICE

"*D*o you need anything before I leave baby? A ginger ale or maybe some crackers?" Nick offered me, standing at the foot of our bed.

I had just dragged myself out of the bathroom from spending the last ten minutes or so throwing up my fucking brains over the toilet.

"No baby, I'm good. I just want to sleep so that I can stop all this damn throwing up." I moaned as I tried to turn on my back, but quickly stopped moving; afraid that the slight motion would cause me to throw up again.

"Alright, call me if you need anything. I'm about to meet up with Ronnie for a few, but I'll be back soon." Nick walked over to me and gave me a kiss on the cheek and left out the room.

I found out a month ago that I was pregnant, and instead

of being excited, I was miserable as hell. Besides me being sick all the damn time, Sky was in a bad state of depression due to that sick ass fuck nigga Gerald kidnapping and raping her again. My momma was going crazy ever since the police told her that they found Damon's body burned up in an alley in Overtown. Not to mention, I also found out that Ronnie is my half-brother.

I never asked Nick or Ronnie anything about what happened with Damon, nor did they offer any information, but I already had a feeling of who was responsible for my brother's death. I admit, I did have mixed feelings about the situation. I mean, he was my brother, but he had done some horrible things to me and others; so, it was only a matter of time before karma caught back up with him.

For a while, when I was younger, Damon used to molest me. It went on for about two years before I said something to my mother. In the beginning, it was just him coming into my room and touching on me. Then, he started making me touch on him. Finally, it escalated to him sticking his dick in me.

The only reason I told my mother was because she washed my clothes and one day she found blood in a pair of my panties and on my bed sheets. I hadn't even begun my period yet, so she already knew the blood came from fucking. She was about to beat the shit out of me when she confronted me about the blood, and that was when I told her the truth about what my brother had been doing to me.

I stood there, crying my eyes out to my mother as I replayed all the sick shit Damon had been doing to me for the last two years, and all she did was call me a liar. The one person who I thought would have my back and could save me, turned on me. Of course, Damon denied it, but he never touched me again after I told my mom.

My mother accused me of being a liar and said that I only blamed those things on my brother because I was fast and already out here fucking up a storm, as she put it. After that, I always felt alone, until I met Sky. Lord knows I didn't mean to keep those things about Damon from her, but I was just scared that he would harm her like he did Celeste and that I would lose her if she would have confronted him.

Now, here it is, and I feel like I lost her anyway. She was already going through enough shit as it is, but what Gerald did to her pushed her over the edge. When Nick first told me what had happened to her, I flipped out and couldn't bring myself to think about what life would be like without my best friend. Then when Ronnie called me over to their house to see her, I was relieved to know that she was alive.

I rushed over there only to be crushed again at the sight of my friend. Her face was fucked up and she looked as if she had the life sucked out of her. I tried my best to talk to her, but she only stared off into space, not responding to anything I was saying to her. That's when I learned that she was in shock from everything. To make matters worse, her momma had regained temporary custody of Imani and I almost lost it!

For a while, I still went to see Sky and tried to convince her to snap out of it so that she could get Imani back, but she still wasn't budging. During everything that was happening, that's when I found out that I was pregnant. Sky and I were supposed to be in college right now, living our fucking lives and having fun, yet we were both stuck in situations that neither of us couldn't seem to get out of.

The only positive thing I had to rely on was Nick. My man had been nothing more than perfect for me. He'd been here since day one and hadn't left my side. When I told him that I was pregnant, he vowed to be here through it all for me and his baby, and so far, he had made good on that promise.

Nick had been the little bit of fresh air that I could grasp during all of that had been going on. Lately, I have been isolating myself in the house dealing with this throwing up 24/7. I was sick and tired of being sick! Besides Nick and Ronnie, no one else knew that I was pregnant. Not even my mother, who still wasn't talking to me because I decided not to go to Damon's funeral.

Finally, able to doze off to sleep, the ringing of my cell phone woke me right back up. I reached over on the night-stand and saw that it was Nick calling me.

"Yes baby" I said as I answered the phone.

"Baby, I need you to get down to Memorial Hospital now; Sky tried to kill herself!" he yelled into the phone.

I became numb as I sat up in the bed. Not needing to hear anything else he had to say, I quickly jumped out of bed and ran downstairs to head to my friend.

Chapter Seven
EVELYN

"Stop all that fucking crying and get yo' ass in the room before I break this belt off in your ass!" I yelled.

Imani cried out even louder as she took her spoiled ass back in the room with Isis' bad ass kids. I was sitting in my living room, irritated as hell because it was hotter than a muthafucka in here. Miami in the month of August wasn't shit to be played with, and this damn landlord was supposed to be here a week ago to fix this fucking air.

"I wish you shut her lil ass up; all that noise while I'm trying to get some damn sleep!" Bobbie grunted as he came out of the bedroom in his drawers, talking shit.

"Why don't you take yo' ass back in the room and put some damn clothes on!" I yelled at his ass as I grabbed my box of Newport's off the table and lit one out of the pack.

"Shut your ass up and go cook me something to eat. Shit, I'm hungry." Bobbie demanded as he turned around and went back into the room, slamming the door behind him.

I wasn't about to fix his ass a got damn thing to eat. Far as I'm concerned, he could starve in this muthafucka! I picked my phone back up off the couch and tried calling Isis' ass again, only to get a recording, telling me that the bitch's voicemail was full. It had been three months since her ass just up and disappeared, leaving her damn kids here with me. I hadn't received not one dollar from her either. If it weren't for me still getting my food stamps and check, I would have probably reported her kids abandoned to the Department of Children and Families; DCF.

Speaking of which, I was able to get temporary custody of Sky's little brat, Imani, which allowed me to keep my benefits and section 8 housing and stop that dumb ass investigating the state had going on with me. I know what folks are thinking; these are my grandkids and I'm a cruel bitch, and they're right too. I was never like this, though. I used to be a woman who had something to look forward to in life. I had dreams and goals, and a man that loved me unconditionally and brought the best out of me.

When I first met Sky's daddy, I already knew that he was too good for me. I was a single mother to Isis, whose daddy had just left us to go be with his wife. So, here I was, living in the projects with my three-year-old daughter, struggling on the system. One day, I was at the bus stop with Isis, waiting on the bus to go to the WIC office, when this guy pulled up along the side of me in his car and asked if I wanted a ride.

I was used to the attention from men back then. I had a body shaped like a Coca-Cola bottle with all the right measurements. All the niggas stayed trying to get this pussy, and before Isis' daddy, I was giving it to them too, if the price was right. Anyway, soon as he pulled up and asked me if I wanted a ride, I immediately gave him straight attitude. It was hot, and I wasn't in the mood for a muthafucka trying to be all up in my face. After turning him down about three times when he kept insisting, I finally said fuck it and decided to just take him up on his offer and let him drop us off. Besides, I had my mace in my bag and blade in my bra, so if he tried any shit, I was gone gut his ass.

On the ride over to the WIC office, I learned that his name was Raymond, Ray for short. He was thirty-two, no kids, which meant no baby momma drama, worked for the county at the water company, and single! Not to mention, he was sexy as hell. He had smooth, chocolate skin, with a clean-shaven head and goatee, and the sexiest smile I ever laid eyes on. This was the first time I was meeting a man that wasn't attached to someone else, and it gave me some type of hope of being able to start over.

That day, Ray stayed with me at the WIC office until my appointment was over, then afterward, he drove us to the grocery store and bought me about two months' worth of groceries. My food stamps weren't scheduled to come until the end of the month anyway, so I was glad about that. Since he bought the food, I invited him over to my place that night for dinner. Ray dropped us off back home after the grocery store and helped me put up the groceries inside, with the promise to come back later that night for dinner.

I felt like a kid in a candy store later that day, but was so nervous to have Ray coming over. Although I lived in the projects, I always kept my place clean and smelling good. I got Isis washed up, fed her some ravioli, and put her little ass to sleep before Ray was scheduled to come over. Even though he seemed to bond with her earlier, I didn't want any interruptions tonight.

After I had got Isis squared away, I fixed a quick meal of spaghetti and garlic cheese toast. Soon as that was done, I put the food on low and went to take a shower. Right when I was done showering and had just finished getting dressed into something more comfortable, Ray was knocking on my door.

I ain't gone lie, that night, I fucked his ass so good that I put that nigga to sleep, snoring! After that night, my life consisted of Ray and Isis. He had not only become a father figure to her, but a good influence on me as well. He encouraged me to take some night classes to get my GED, which I did, and I also take up a trade to get my CNA license as well.

Six months into dating, Ray moved us out of the projects and into his place. He stayed in a two-bedroom apartment in the North Miami area, which was way better than the shit I was living in. I was all about my man and our little family. A year into dating, we found out that I was pregnant again.

Ray loved Isis just like she was biologically his, but he was happy as hell to be having a baby of his own. Even his momma, Ms. Betty, who I met when we got serious, was happy to be having her first grandchild. The whole nine months, I wanted for nothing and was catered to. Ray just wanted me to stay home and relax and take care of Isis while he handled the rest.

Right when I gave birth, he proposed to me that night in the hospital and I gladly accepted. After Sky was born, things went right back to normal with us. Ray was still working and taking care of us, and I got a job at a nursing home, putting my CNA license to use. Ms. Betty offered to watch the girls so that we wouldn't have to pay for daycare while we both worked.

I had a job, not depending on the system anymore, a good ass man who was now my fiancé, and two healthy, beautiful daughters. Life was good and I was blessed, up until I got hurt on the job and they decided to let me go. I ended up having a slip and fall at work and hurt my back and broke my hip.

At first, they granted me a leave of absence while I did rehab, but eventually, they had to let me go because they needed somebody to fill my position. You already know I filed a lawsuit against their asses after that! While rehabbing my back and hip, my doctor prescribed me some pain pills to help ease some of the pain I was now dealing with. All the while, Ray was picking up the slack at home with tending to the girls since I wasn't able to move around as much.

As time went on, I started to become more and more dependent on the Vicodin, Tramadol, and Percocet. When my doctor started realizing that I was requesting refills quicker than I should, he took me off them, but it was too late because I was already hooked. No longer able to get the meds, I decided to try the street drugs instead to help me with the pain. That's when coke came into play.

I had no intentions of getting hooked, but it seemed like the coke was the only thing that helped with the pain; then when I would come down from my high, I would start hurting again. Over time, Ray started to take notice that shit wasn't right with me anymore, especially when my back and hip had gotten better. The house began to be unkempt, I wasn't looking after the girls like I should, and would leave him to do things like bathe them and feed them.

When I didn't want to be bothered, I would have him take their ass to his momma's place. Shortly after, the bill money started coming up short without the bills being paid, and that's when he finally confronted me and asked if I using drugs. By then, I was well into snorting, so me stopping was out of the question. Ray became so fucking frustrated that he wouldn't let me get my hands on any of the money he was bringing in and also took me off the bank account.

Things started to get rough for me when I didn't have the means to supply my habit anymore, and the lawsuit was still pending and taking its damn time to come through. One Friday evening, the girls were at Ray's momma's house and I was home, feening for a hit.

"Ray, I swear to fucking God, if you don't give me some damn money so I can go and get me some dope, I'll take my ass out there and

sell pussy for that shit!" I threatened, screaming and shaking like a real live dope head.

I had never done it before, but I was just that desperate to take my ass to the streets and trick.

"Evelyn, you don't mean that shit." Ray said, waving me off, not taking me seriously.

"Oh, you think I'm bullshitting? Watch this shit nigga!"

I got up off the couch and headed towards the door to leave; by any means, I was determined to get high that night.

"Where the hell you think you going?" Ray yelled, running past me to the door to block me from leaving out.

"Get the fuck out of my way! I told yo' ass that I'm going to get me some dope and that's exactly what I mean." I tried pushing past him.

"Look at you! You have completely become a fucking dope head! You don't take care of the kids, this house; all the ambition you once had is out the fucking window! This ain't the woman you are, Evelyn!" Ray was standing in my face, shaking my shoulders.

"Muthafucka you don't know the real me! The real me was the street bitch you met standing at the bus stop that day! The real me was staying in the projects, paying my twenty-three dollars a month rent and getting my two-hundred dollars a month in food stamps! The real me would fuck a bitch's husband, boyfriend, or brother, just to get what I want! That's the real me, so stop thinking we this perfect fucking partridge family!" I lost control as I had tears coming out my eyes.

I was tired of always having temporary happiness and getting my hopes up high, only to be let down. Ray pulled me into this arms, holding me while I cried in his chest. Even though I was crying and had just said how I felt, I still wanted to get high and had plans on doing so.

"Baby, don't say that. You just had a hard life and I have been doing everything that I possibly can to make sure you don't go back down that road." Ray said to me while I was still in his arms.

All that shit he was saying was going in one ear and out the other. My mind started wandering on how I could get my hands on some coke. With no money and Ray not letting me leave out the house, I knew the only way I could get some was if he went and got it for me. That's when I went into hustle mode.

"Baby, I'm sorry. I know that I have been slacking lately, but I feel like everything that I have been working so hard for has slipped away from me. I get a good job, only to get hurt and fired from it. Rehab doesn't seem to be working, and the constant pain that I'm in is unbearable! Then my fucking asshole doctor thinks that I can deal with this pain on my own and eventually get better, but I can't baby, which is why I had to find something stronger and better to help me. Trust me when I say, I'm not hooked on coke. I just need the pain to stop!" I was now crying so hard that I had snot coming out my damn nose.

I know Ray thought that I was crying because I was sincere, but shit, all I wanted was a hit! We both stood there, with Ray still consoling me.

"Okay baby, I'll get it for you this one time, but after this, I'm going to get you some real help." he finally spoke, agreeing to what I wanted in the first place.

Needless to say, that was far from the only time Ray got

dope for me. Matter of fact, I convinced his ass to start using with me so that we could be 'as one in everything that we do', as I put it. I knew Ray loved me with his soul and was weak for me. We both became functional addicts together.

He still got up and went to work every day and I went back to trying to take care of the house and the girls just as I had before. What caused us to take a bad turn, was when the nursing home that I was suing finally decided to settle with me. We settled on the ten thousand they offered me, even though I was suing for more.

I didn't give a damn though; all I saw was more money for Ray and me to continue to get high together. Once I got the money, I planned a big coke and fuck fest for us that weekend. I sent Isis and Sky to Ms. Betty's apartment, telling her that me and her son were having a romantic weekend to ourselves, and of course, she was more than happy to watch the girls.

That weekend, Ray and I got so fucking high and fucked up, that we lost touch with everything else outside of our apartment. All we did was snort dope, fuck, snort dope some more, eat, and snort dope some more. We didn't leave our place that entire weekend. I even had the dope boy bring us a huge stash of shit just so we didn't have to leave to cop.

We were so fucked up that we must have blacked out because I woke up to a banging sound on the front door. At first, I thought I was hearing shit, but when I heard the banging again, and this time, someone saying they were the police, I struggled to get myself up. I made my way over to the door and opened it up to find two police officers standing there, along with Ms. Betty and my kids.

"Oh my God, Evelyn! What happened to you?" I heard Ms. Betty ask me.

I had no idea what the fuck she was talking about.

"Ma'am, we received a call from Ms. Robinson here saying that you and her son had not been responding to her calls or answering your door for a week, and that she has your kids." one of the officers spoke to me.

A week? What the fuck! I thought to myself as I was still standing there, trying to comprehend. I had no idea what time or day it was. The only thing I could remember was Ray and I getting fucked up together.

Ray! "Oh shit!" I yelled as I turned around and stumbled back into the living room.

Ray was sprawled out on the living room floor on his stomach.

"Ray," I slurred as I bent down to shake him. "Ray!" I repeated louder when I didn't get a response from him. I turned him over onto his back, and his eyes were open, staring straight up at the ceiling.

"Oh my God, Ray!" I cried out.

I didn't even notice that his momma, the police, and my kids were standing behind me in the living room. That was the day my life turned into the hell that it was today. I blamed myself, and still do, for getting Ray hooked on dope. I was so angry and bitter at the world and everything in it. I felt so guilty that I distanced myself from all things that reminded me of him, including Sky.

That's why she went to live with his mom and I treated her the way I did. Looking at her is like looking at Ray. She was his identical twin and a constant reminder of how I was the one responsible for his death. I purposely detached myself from my child so I wouldn't have to accept what I had done. By me becoming cold hearted and letting myself go, that made it easy for me to do.

Ray was the only man I loved and loved me back unconditionally, and I fucked that up. Lord knows I think about him every day and wonder what life would be like if he were here, but like I said, I fucked that up a long time ago and this is who I am...always have been.

Chapter Eight

NICK

I sat in the hospital waiting room, consoling Katrice as she cried on my lap. Earlier, Ronnie was out with me, looking at some property for the overnight daycare center I was trying to open. This was one of my many investments. Now that we were out of the game, I could put my money to use with going legit.

The daycare was to help those that work overnight or want to work overnight, but have a hard time getting someone to watch their kids. My cousin, Sharon, who is more like a big sister to me, is a social worker and she's going to run everything for me since she's already familiar with the field. I'm just going to put up the cash and fund everything else. Anyway, Ronnie got a phone call from Ms. Mary saying that the ambulance was taking Sky to the hospital. The only question Ronnie asked was what hospital they were taking her to and we made our way here, speeding.

When we got here, Ms. Mary was already waiting in the waiting room, crying. That's when she told us that she went upstairs to check on Sky and that she was in the bathroom, slumped on the toilet with a razor in her hand and blood running from her wrist. Ronnie ended up punching the wall and fucked up his hand in the process. He was in the back now as well, getting that shit looked at. I called Katrice and told her what happened, and of course, she came running.

Although she and Sky hadn't officially made up since that blowout they had, she was still by her side, no matter what.

"Ms. Mary, why don't you have a seat; you been pacing the floor since we got here." I said to her as she was walking back and forth in the waiting room.

"I can't baby. I feel like this is my fault." she said as she wiped her eyes with her handkerchief.

"Ms. Mary, this is far from being your fault. Sky hasn't been herself since...you know" I said to her, not wanting to bring up the Gerald incident.

"I know, but I should have been watching her; that's what I'm there for." she cried.

Katrice jumped up from my lap and ran over to console Ms. Mary. For the short time we all had known her, Ms. Mary had become like family to us. I guess you can say she's like the grandmother we never had. I sat there and just stared at those two holding one another and crying. If only Sky would allow herself to see the love that we all have for her.

Chapter Nine

RONNIE

I was sitting in the chair next to Sky's hospital bed with my head down as tears fell down my face. I didn't give a fuck who saw me or thought that I was a pussy, because at this point, my woman was not only trying to leave me, but leave this world period and I couldn't have that. I sat back up in the chair and winced in pain. I ended up punching the wall when I found out that Sky tried to kill herself, and broke my fucking hand; which resulted in me getting a cast on it.

I refused to take the pain medicine they prescribed be, because I wanted to be here and when Sky woke up, and I didn't need shit interfering with that. Scooting the chair closer to the side of her bed, I grabbed hold of Sky's hand and kissed on the bandage that was wrapped around her wrist that she cut.

"I can't believe you tried to leave Imani and me baby." I said in a low tone, talking to Sky as she laid there.

The doctors told me that she lost a lot of blood and that they had to do a quick blood transfusion for her, which was successful. Now she was asleep from the morphine they gave her for the pain.

"I told you that I was getting our baby back, but I need you here with me bae. Please don't give up on us. I promised you that no one else was going to hurt you, and I meant that shit!" I cried out.

Watching Sky lay up in this hospital bed was eating through my soul. I felt like half of me was slipping, just as she was, and there wasn't shit I could do about it.

Chapter Ten

SKY

I opened my eyes and looked around; and saw that I was in my old bed at my grandmother's apartment and sat up. Thank God it was all a dream, I thought to myself as I got out of the bed and walked out of my bedroom into the living room. I smiled when I saw Granny sitting on the couch, staring in the direction of the television, which wasn't turned on.

"Granny, you wouldn't believe the dream I had; I swear it felt so real!" I said as I came around the couch to face her. She looked up at me with tears in her eyes.

"What's wrong granny?" I asked, alarmed as I went and took a seat next to her on the couch.

"You lost your faith baby." she answered, looking at me.

"What do you mean I lost my faith?" I asked her, confused.

"You tried to take your own life. You gave up on Imani and you're *pushing that man who loves you so much away. You gave up." she explained, still crying.*

"Granny, how did you know about my dream?" I asked her.

Everything she had just said was what I had dreamt, but what I didn't understand was how she knew about Imani because I didn't have a real-life daughter, only in my dream.

"You weren't dreaming baby; it was all real." Granny confirmed.

"So you mean to tell me—" I began to say.

"Yes, everything did happen and I did go on to glory." Granny said, nodding her head as if she knew what I was about to ask.

I started crying as I reached over and hugged her.

"I missed you so much Granny! Everything has been so messed up since you left me." I cried into her arms.

I missed her so much! Just being able to touch and smell her again gave me comfort.

"I know things have been hard baby, but you gotta be strong. You have a beautiful baby out here that needs you, and so does Ronnie." she said as she pulled me away from her and stared at me.

This was the first time that I noticed granny looking so beautiful and peaceful. She had on the light pink dress she was buried in, with her long hair in curls, cascading down her face.

"Granny, it's too much. It seems like every time I think things are getting better, they don't. It doesn't matter how hard I try or how good of a mother and person I try to be, life just still hits me hard. I'm so worn down that I feel like things will be better off without me; there's just no more fight left in me. Please just let me stay here with you where I won't have to deal with the pain and life's disappointments anymore." I cried out.

"Listen to me Sky; you are much stronger than you think! God has a great plan for you, but you have to be able to show Him that you can handle anything He gives you baby. I know things have been hard for you, but believe me when I say you are going to be one of His soldiers with a testimony." Granny comforted me.

"But if you're here, and I'm able to talk to you, then that must mean I didn't make it." I took notice.

"No, I'm here to tell you that now is not your time, and to also tell you that you need to go back and get Imani and help your mom too." Granny replied.

"Help my mom? Granny, that woman hates me and you know it! She didn't even want me and treated me like a dog when you left and I had to go live with her!" I explained.

There was no way I was helping someone who hated me for no fucking reason.

"Your mother doesn't hate you, she just feels guilty about your daddy, that's all. She's been fighting those demons ever since he passed."

"Feel guilty about my daddy? Granny, what does she feel guilty about?" I asked, more confused now than ever.

"You need to have that conversation with her. But first, you must get yourself together, get Imani back, and let Ronnie be there for you because you can't do this alone. I love you baby and I'll always be here." Granny hugged me one last time and vanished.

My eyes felt heavy as I fluttered them open. The light from the ceiling caused me to squint. Finally, able to open them fully, I looked over to my right and saw Ronnie halfway laying on my bed with his head while still sitting in the chair. I reached over and grabbed his hand, squeezing it. Ronnie must have felt my touch because his head shot up and he looked at me.

"Hi baby." I whispered, starring at him with a faint smile.

Chapter Eleven

ISIS

"*D*amn, right there nigga. Fuck you hitting this shit!" I moaned out as dude was tearing my pussy up from the back.

Truthfully, his dick was small and whack as fuck, but I needed the money, so I had to do whatever it took to get it. If that involved lying to this man, just so that it could make him hurry up and cum, and that I could get the fuck out of here, then so be it. After a few more pumps, his fat ass grunted and started shaking, which let me know that he was done. Quickly jumping up, I reached down to the floor and grabbed my clothes and started putting them on. *Fuck this shit, I'll shower when I get back to the room.* I thought to myself as I got dressed.

Soon as I was done dressing, I went and stood at the foot of the bed in front of the trick with my hand out; he knew what time it was.

"Why don't you stay for a while and chill with me Tiffany? Shit, you always in a rush to leave after I tear that pussy up." he laughed, calling me by the fake name I gave him.

"Nigga, please! You couldn't tear my pussy up if you had a bigger dick and instructions on how to! Just give me my money so that I can go, and you can get back home to yo' wife." I said with attitude, with my hand still out, waiting for him to pay me my two hundred dollars he owed me.

I guess he was pissed about what I said. He reached down on the floor for his pants, snatched them up, pulled his wallet out and threw the money at me. Bending down, I snatched it up, counting ten twenty dollar bills. Satisfied, I headed towards the door to leave.

"Same time next week?" I turned around and asked him before walking out.

"Naw, I need some new pussy." he responded, trying to get slick.

I just laughed as I walked out the motel room and slammed the door. He was in his feelings, but trust me when I say, his ass would be blowing my phone up next week, feening for this pussy. I walked a couple of doors down to my room, unlocked the door, and let myself in.

Locking the door behind me, I leaned my back against the door, closed my eyes, and let out an exasperated breath. I was beyond tired and wanted nothing more than to take a hot bath while soaking in some Epsom salt, and go to sleep. Today I tricked with a total of seven different dudes and my pussy was beyond sore!

"You done for the night?"

I opened my eyes to see Gerald coming in the room from out of the bathroom, limping with his cane.

"Yeah, I'mma just take a bath and hit the sack." I responded as I started to walk past him, heading to the bathroom.

He grabbed hold of my arm, stopping me in my tracks.

"You already know how this shit goes; put the money on the bed first." he ordered.

Sucking my teeth and snatching my arm away, I opened my purse and pulled out five hundred dollars and handed it to Gerald.

Snatching the money out of my hand, he counted it and looked back up at me.

"This it?" his ass had the nerve to ask.

"What you mean is that it?" I shot back at him, annoyed, with my hand on my hip.

"Yo' ass been gone all damn day and only came back with five hundred dollars? Shit, I know how yo' ass roll Isis, and knowing you, you probably cuffing the rest."

Damn right I was cuffing, but I wasn't about to let this nigga know that shit. I wasn't as dumb as Gerald thought I was. Every time I got money for fucking, I always skimmed some off the top and gave the rest to him. There was no way in hell I was about to give his ass all my fucking money, especially when I was the one doing all the fucking work.

"Gerald, ain't nobody cuffing shit!" I lied. "I gave you all I made and that's it. Now, I'm going to go take a bath and soak in some Epson salt."

I walked into the bathroom and locked the door behind me. Turning on the water in the tub to fill it up, I reached into the medicine cabinet and grabbed the box of Epson salt out. Once I poured some in the bath water, I undressed and got inside. The water was extremely hot, just how I liked it.

Satisfied with the amount of water now in the tub, I turned it off and leaned back on the base of the bath tub with my eyes closed. This was not how shit was supposed to be. Right now, I should have a pocket full of money and have my ass far away from here, out of the state of Florida. Instead, I was in a shitty ass motel in West Palm Beach, Florida, damn near broke, fucking for money, with Gerald's ass acting as if he was my damn pimp.

I knew I shouldn't have agreed to be a part of that dumb ass plan with kidnapping Sky and having Ronnie pay ransom for her with him. Not only did that shit not work, but we ended up not getting paid and having to leave Miami because we knew Ronnie would be gunning for Gerald. I decided to leave with him too since I didn't know if Sky knew that I was in on it or not. To this day, I still hadn't heard anything from her and was scared to reach out to her. That day, when Gerald hit her truck and we crashed in a ditch, I climbed out the truck without her noticing and hauled ass. At the time, my head was fucked up from when I hit the dashboard on impact, and I ended up having to go to the hospital to get stitches on my forehead, which I still had the scar to show.

Gerald took Sky back to his duck off spot in Overtown, while I laid low at his place, waiting for his call, letting me know that everything was handled and that he had the money, but that shit never happened. Instead, I got a call later from his ass telling me to come and pick him up. This muthafucka was hiding in an abandoned building, sweating and bleeding with three bullet holes in his ass. One in the shoulder, one in the side, and another one in the right leg.

When I got there, Gerald urged me to take him to the hospital here in West Palm Beach because he didn't want to risk running into Gerald or his people. I honestly thought that he was going to bleed out all over my back seat with the amount of blood he was losing before we even made it to the hospital since West Palm Beach was almost an hour drive from Miami.

When we finally made it there, Gerald gave the hospital a bogus ass story, saying that he was robbed and didn't know who it was that robbed him. I stayed by his ass the entire time, too afraid to be alone at that point since Ronnie was still out there. I knew what he was capable of doing and the pull he had, so if Ronnie was going to get me, he was definitely getting Gerald's ass too!

Lucky for Gerald, the bullet that hit him in the shoulder and leg passed right through, but he wasn't as lucky with the one that hit him on the side. It was an inch away from hitting the main artery, which would have killed him. Gerald had to have surgery in order to remove it and spent a week in the hospital.

The entire time, I stayed right there with him, which I could just kick my ass for right now. I should have hauled ass when I had the chance and gotten out of dodge altogether. Now, I was stuck in this shit with no real money to leave. I know I couldn't go back to my Miami or my momma's house. Shit, I already knew she was pissed because I left my kids with her and no money, but I honestly didn't give a fuck about that.

What I needed to find out thought, was if Sky knew that I was a part of the plan with Gerald kidnapping her or not.

Chapter Twelve

RONNIE

I was sitting outside of my lawyer's office in the parking lot in my car. I had just met with him in regards to the next step we were about to take on me getting Imani back. I swear all this court shit just wasn't for me. This wasn't how I dealt with things when it came to handling my own, but I was stressed like a muthafucka!

I felt like I had no control over what was going on in my life anymore. You would think I would be living peacefully and enjoying being out of the game, but this straight life stressed me out more than selling dope. My lawyer was able to get the custody hearing pushed up a month from now, which was good since it was family court, but I don't think I could wait that long to get my baby girl.

Since Imani had been at Evelyn's, I'd been having eyes on her place, making sure no foul shit was going on. All I got so far was that Imani was there with some other little kids and that's it. Evelyn had even pulled my baby out of daycare, so basically, she was home all day with Evelyn's sorry ass. That would help my court case for trying to get custody of Imani.

I had the finances to support her and a stable environment, but the problem I knew would come into play would be Sky. After she had woke up that day in the hospital, they admitted her to the psych ward and she's still in there. I know for a fact Sky isn't crazy, but the way she's been acting has these folks thinking she is. Sky doesn't say shit; she just sits there and stares off into space. The doctor said she has a bad case of depression, which resulted in them putting her on meds to control it.

It took everything in me not to break down every day I go there and visit with her. I talk to her and try my hardest to convince my baby to snap out of it so that I could take her home, but she never responds to me. Honestly, I don't even know if there was anything else I could do to help Sky right now. I leaned my head back on the headrest and sighed loudly.

Think Ronnie, there has to be some shit you can do to start fixing this whole situation I thought to myself. My mind was racing and after a few minutes, a thought came to mind. I cranked my car up and pulled out of the parking lot, heading towards Evelyn's house.

It pissed me off to even think this, but I knew that it would work with her ass. Evelyn was a money hungry bitch who would do anything for a come up, especially if she doesn't have to get off her ass. I was on my way to her house to make her an offer I knew she wouldn't refuse, and at the same time, would help me get Imani back.

Lost in my thoughts, I didn't even notice how quickly I got to her house on the other side of town in Miami Gardens. I pulled up and cut my car off. Reaching into my secret compartment in my middle armrest, I pulled my gun out and placed it in the front of my waist in my pants under my shirt. I grabbed my phone and cut the recorder on, then placed it in the front of my pants pocket. Getting out, I took notice of my surroundings before walking up to the front door and knocking on it. I banged on it loud, hoping this bitch heard me and hurried her ass up to open this muthafucka.

Knocking again, because she didn't answer the first time, Evelyn finally opened the door.

"What the fuck you want?" She opened the door, smoking a cigarette, looking at me with her damn nose turned up.

Shit, I should be the one with my nose turned up; this bitch smelled a little tart!

"Look Evelyn, I didn't come over here to start no shit. I just want us to be able to talk and solve this shit before going into court. Can I come in?" I asked sincerely.

I knew I had to keep calm and play this shit right if I was about to leave out of here with my baby. Evelyn stared at me for a few seconds like she was sizing me up as she blew smoke out of her mouth. Flicking her cigarette past me and onto the ground outside, she moved to the side without saying anything and opened the door wider to let me inside.

Stepping inside, the strong smell of piss mixed with funk hit my nose. The place was also a fucking mess with dishes piled up in the sink, pizza boxes open on the coffee table, newspapers and trash were thrown everywhere, and ashtrays filled with cigarette butts. *This bitch is beyond nasty!* I stayed standing by the door, not wanting to sit on that nasty ass couch.

"What is it that you need to say because the last time I saw you, you called me a fucked up bitch who only wanted Imani for the benefits of the state." she said, taking a seat on the couch and lighting up another cigarette.

I did go in on her ass the last time we were in court when the judge ruled for her to have temporary custody of Imani. Taking a deep breath to contain my anger, I spoke. "I'm sorry about that. A lot has been going on and at that time, I was pissed." I explained.

"Whatever. What you want, Mr. Dope Man Ronnie?" Evelyn smirked, looking at me.

"What?" I scrunched up my face.

"Yeah, I know who you are, and I damn sure have plans on letting the courts know that my granddaughter's life would be in danger living with a well-known drug dealer." she laughed.

"Naw, you think you know me—"

"Cut the shit, nigga! I know exactly who the fuck you are. Sky's ass lucked up fucking with yo' ass and having Imani from you, so unless you here to talk money, you can save that other shit you trying to spit to me." Evelyn cut me off from talking.

"Where's Imani?" I asked, looking around.

"Her ass in the back room sleeping since I just tore that ass up with all that damn crying she was doing." she replied casually like she didn't have a care in the world with announcing that she put her hands on my child.

It took everything in me not to pull my gun out and shoot this bitch right between her fucking eyes.

"How much you want Evelyn?" I asked, getting straight to the point as to why I was here in the first place.

I knew this bitch wouldn't turn down any type of money, and she confirmed that when she said that if I wasn't here to talk about money, I could bounce.

"See, that's what I'm talking about! Money talks and bull-shit walks." she said eagerly. "Give me fifty thousand and you can have the brat with no problems from me." she proposed.

"Shit, I know you got it." Evelyn added.

I stood there staring at her ass as if she lost her got damn mind. I don't give a fuck if I had the fifty thousand, plus more, I wasn't about to give it to this bitch!

"Let's be realistic here Evelyn. You know damn well I'm not about to give yo' ass fifty thousand dollars. You also don't know about me because if you do, then you wouldn't even fix your mouth to ask for that amount of money." I stated as I stared at her.

Right then, I took my phone out of my pocket and stopped the recording.

"What the fuck is that?" Evelyn asked, noticing what I had just done.

"That was me recording yo' stupid ass trying to extort money out of me to get my own child." I held the phone up.

"You the one that just asked me how much!" she yelled.

"So what, I can easily have my lawyer argue that I was asking you how much you needed to care for Imani while she's in your care."

"You know what, fuck you, Sky, and that cry baby ass brat y'all got!" Evelyn yelled out.

Before she could say anything else out her greasy ass mouth, I ran over to where she was and wrapped my hand around her throat. With her eyes bulging and her trying to remove my hand from around her neck, I squeezed harder. I heard a door open from behind me. Still choking Evelyn, I turned my head to see some dude coming out of the hallway bathroom.

"What the fuck going on!" he yelled as he saw me choking Evelyn's ass out.

I pulled my gun out from the front of my pants with my free hand, the other one still wrapped around Evelyn's fat ass neck, I turned around and pointed it at this nigga.

"Sit yo' fuck ass down before I put one in yo' shit." I threatened.

Buddy held his hands up in the air in a surrender stance as he stumbled his ass over to the couch where we were and took a seat. Turning my attention back to Evelyn, who was still gasping for air, I finally released my grip from around her throat and stood back.

"Now, this is how this shit gone go. You gone call the bitch ass lawyer of yours and let her know that you don't want temporary custody of Imani anymore, with no fucking explanation given. Then your ass better not show up to fucking court either. I'm taking my baby and getting the fuck out of here, and you better not even try to be on some slick shit about it. You claim you heard about me; well, try me bitch and you'll see just how I get down." I warned her ass while aiming my gun at her face.

Evelyn's ass was just sitting there, staring at me, shaking with tears in her eyes. Seeing the fear she displayed caused me to smile.

"You got this shit?" I questioned just to make sure we had the same understanding.

Evelyn nodded her head up and down quickly.

"I can't hear shit!" I yelled in her face.

"Bitch, open yo' mouth and talk!" dude blurted out, sitting next to her.

I had to contain myself from laughing at what the fuck he just said. Even he had more sense than her ass.

"Yes, I hear you. I'll do everything you just said." Evelyn spoke, fumbling over her words.

Looking at her for a few more seconds, I put my gun back in the front of my pants.

"Good, now where the fuck is my baby?" I asked.

"She's right here in this room." Buddy jumped up from the couch and started to walk towards the back.

"Nigga, sit yo' ass down! I ain't ask you to go get my shorty!" I yelled, pulling his ass back by the back of his neck.

At this point, no other man could be around Imani, but me and muthafuckas I trusted; which was very few.

"I'm sorry man. I was just trying to help." he said, running back over to the couch.

I walked into the room he was going towards and opened the door. The smell of piss hit me even harder, letting me know that the smell originated from here. The fucking room was so damn messy with clothes, toys, shoes, and other shit was thrown all over the place. The television was on some damn cartoon.

I walked over to the bunk beds in the corner of the room, and saw my baby curled up in a fetal position on the bottom bunk. The sight of my Imani caused my heart to skip a beat. I bent down to pick her up and noticed that she had on wet underwear, which was most likely piss. I took my shirt off, wrapped her in it, and picked her up. Imani woke up and smiled when she saw that it was me.

Evelyn and old boy were still sitting their asses in the same spot, staring at me when I came out of the room, holding Imani in my arms.

"You see this little girl right here?" I said, positioning Imani so that they could see her face. "She just saved y'all fucking life. If either one of your asses comes near her or Sky again in life, I'll kill both you bitches and drop yo' body off to the morgue my-damn-self."

I kicked the raggedy ass screen door open with my foot, breaking that shit off the hinges, and walked back outside to my car. I took my keys out of my pocket and hit the alarm, unlocking the car, and opened the back door, laying Imani down on the back seat. With my shirt still wrapped around her, I buckled the seat belt and went around to the driver's side and got in. Cranking my car up, I pulled off, heading home with my daughter.

Chapter Thirteen

GERALD

"**F**uck!" I yelled out in pain as I changed the dressing on my wound on my side.

Isis' ass was supposed to be here doing this shit, but she called herself having to meet up with some dude early this morning for a quick fuck for some cash. I already know that hoe was being sneaky and not bringing me back all the money she was making, but right now, there wasn't shit that I could do about it. That day when Ronnie and the rest of those fuck niggas rolled up in my spot and started blazing, I was lucky I got my black ass out of there with only three holes in my ass instead of being six feet deep.

When they barged in my shit and started shooting, I was in the kitchen getting Sky something to eat when I was hit. My body jerked from the bullets hitting me and I immediately hit the floor. Until this day, I know it was by the grace of God that I was still able to slip away without them bitch ass niggas noticing it. At first, I was trying to wreck my brain on how the fuck Ronnie knew where to find me and where I had Sky, because knew one knew where my duck off spot was. Then I remembered I had one of my pussy workers met me there one day to do a re-up from me when I didn't have time to get to him. It was all good though; I had something for his rat ass, right along with Ronnie.

The only person I could call at the time was Isis, which I did, and she came and got my ass and had been with me since then. I put in her head that if she didn't stick with me, Ronnie would find her and kill her ass because he found out that she was in on the shit with me kidnapping Sky. Truthfully, I didn't even know if it was true that he knew about Isis being involved with the plan to help me kidnap Sky or not, nor did I give a fuck.

Right now, Isis was my only hustle until I came up with a reclusive plan and got back on my feet. So, having her sell pussy and me collecting on it was how we were surviving at the moment. As for now, we were out here in West Palm Beach, laying low, staying in this raggedy ass motel. After I was done cleaning my wound and changing the dressing, I limped out the bathroom, back into the room.

Sitting on the bed, breathing heavy from the pain, I reached over into the nightstand drawer and pulled out my pain reliever. Pouring the coke onto the tray, I picked up the rolled-up dollar bill and started snorting. Once all the coke was gone, I leaned back against the headboard and closed my eyes as my high started to take effect. I used to dabble in a little coke here and there every now and again, but now this shit had become a habit.

Since I wasn't about to stay in the hospital like the doctor suggested and go back to be seen about, the coke was the only thing that helped with the pain I was constantly in. Every day when Isis would bring back money, I used half the shit to cop. It was easy to find a regular dope boy up here in West Palm Beach, so I had him deliver here at the motel instead of me going out to him.

"Damn nigga, this all the fuck you do!" I opened my eyes to see Isis standing at the foot of the bed with her hands on her hips, looking pissed.

I was so fucked up right now that I didn't even hear her ass come in. Although I was getting tired of her fucking attitude and slick ass mouth, she looked good as fuck standing there in that short ass skirt and crop top, showing off her sexy ass frame.

"Man don't start." I said in a low tone, but loud enough for her to hear me.

"Don't start? Lately, all your ass been doing is stuffing the money I'm trying to make up your fucking nose! The plan was to get this money so that we could get the fuck out of here so we could start over somewhere fresh with you running shit!" she yelled.

Yeah, that was the initial plan, but little did her ass know, the only part of it that she was going to be involved in was helping me get enough money to get up out of here and buy some bricks to start me off. I had plans to move to North Carolina and work my way up to the top, and Isis wasn't going to be anywhere in the picture when I do. There was no way that I would be able to make moves in Florida anymore, not even with my Haitian connects on my guns.

Ronnie owned all this shit, and I knew in order for me to get to him and get rid of his ass once and for all, I would have to have my own muscle.

"Aye, check this out. I don't need yo' ass coming in here and telling me what the fuck we trying to do when I'm the muthafucka that's handling all that. The only thing you need to worry about is doing your part, now come over here and suck this dick." I demanded as I grabbed my dick out of my basketball shorts and started stroking it.

Each time I got high, I also got horny as hell. Since I've been shot, the only thing Isis' ass had been doing was giving me head. Although her shit was certified, I still needed to be up in some pussy. Isis just stood there staring at me as I stroked my shit, with nothing but lust in her eyes. I swear this girl was a fucking freak hoe. Here she was, standing here with her mouthwatering, ready to jump on my dick when she just came back from fucking and sucking another nigga.

This is why this bitch was only beneficial to me when it counted. I would never wife her ass. Isis pulled her shirt over her head and pulled down her skirt and panties at the same time. She walked over to my side of the bed and grabbed my dick out of my hand and put it in her mouth.

"That's right, take care of this dick." I said as I grabbed

the top of her head as her lips were caressing and sucking on the head of my dick.

Isis was swirling her tongue around as she jacked my dick up and down in her mouth. My damn toes started curling from this shit! She knew I liked my shit sloppy, so she started spitting on my dick, making slurping sounds as she put all eight and a half inches of meat in her mouth without so much as a gag.

Massaging my balls, she continued to give me head; I knew I was about to explode.

"Get up and ride this fucking dick." I commanded as I pulled her head up by her hair.

Isis sat up and climbed her way on top of me and straddled me.

"Ouch, be careful. You know a nigga still sore." I winced out in pain.

"I'm sorry daddy." Isis licked my ear as she slid down on my dick.

Her pussy felt like so warm when I slid in. For a bitch who stayed fucking niggas, you would expect her pussy to be garbage and loose, but it wasn't. Isis' pussy stayed tight and wet every time I fucked her. I don't know what trick her ass used to keep it that way, but that shit worked.

I grabbed both of her fat ass cheeks and started bouncing them up and down on my dick as she started riding my shit.

"Yeah bitch, squeeze those pussy muscles tight." I ordered as I pumped in and out of her fast.

Isis leaned up and cupped her titties, putting her nipples

in her mouth, sucking on them as she continued to ride my dick like she was in a fucking rodeo. I wanted to feel this pussy from the back, so I told her to get on all fours.

I started fucking the dog shit out of her from the back as I pulled on her hair.

"Yes daddy, right there!" Isis moaned out, which caused me to go even harder.

I grabbed hold of her hips with both of my hands and plunged hard as hell in her pussy. I felt my nut rising as her juices were sliding down my dick. Getting ready to explode, I held on to her tighter as I started going faster.

"Oh shit, damn Sky!" I yelled out as I unloaded all my cum in her pussy.

Between getting high and busting this big ass nut, I was out of commission right now. I fell back onto the bed, trying to catch my breath.

"So you just gone call me that bitch's name while you fucking me?" I heard Isis yell.

Right now, I didn't give a fuck if I called her ass the Queen of England's name. I was taking my ass to sleep... and that's exactly what I did.

Chapter Fourteen

SKY

$\mathcal{I}$ was sitting in the chair at Jackson Mental Hospital, staring out the window. I don't even know how long I had been here and really didn't care. All I wanted was to be left alone, away from everyone and anything from the outside world. If that involved me being in here, then so be it. When I first awakened in the hospital that day, it really was my intention to try and do as my grandma had asked of me when she came to me, and be strong. But, finding out that Imani was still in my mother's care and feeling the effects of the pain I was in physically from what Gerald had done to me, overpowered any intentions I had. I had to get twenty stitches on my asshole due to the tearing from when he raped me. I had a concussion, my nose was broken, and my ribs were still fucked up from when Damon whooped my ass before.

I wouldn't have wished everything I was going through on anybody, not even the muthafuckas that did it to me. Then there was Isis. I just knew my sister was somewhere dead because of me. I stayed silent to all those who tried to get me to talk. From Ronnie to Ms. Mary, the doctors, nurses and even Katrice when she visited me in the hospital.

I was tired of hearing folks telling me how I needed to pull myself together and how they knew how I felt. That was straight bullshit! None of their asses knew how the fuck I was feeling. Here I was, not even twenty years old yet, and already going through shit that people twice my age hadn't been through. Why did God hate me so much?

I know that I've done things in the beginning of my life that He didn't approve of with fucking, smoking, drinking, and so on, but that still wouldn't be enough for Him to allow me to go through all the shit I was dealing with. Losing my grandmother, losing Ronnie, getting raped, having my own momma hate me, getting abused and raped by Damon, only to have Ronnie come back into my life again when it was all too late.

I was damaged goods and didn't deserve to be in his or Imani's life. When Ronnie comes to visit me, I actually listen to everything he says to me, even though he thinks I don't. I knew he got a DNA test and it confirmed that Imani was his, which was a relief, but I also learned of the bullshit he was going through with Evelyn and fighting for custody of Imani.

He begged me to get it together and help him get our daughter back, but I just couldn't. No matter how bad I wanted to, I couldn't bring myself to deal with all the heartache, pain, and disappointment repeatedly. I loved Imani and Ronnie more than anything. That's why I decided to stay locked away and let them eventually go on with their lives without me; they were better off.

Imani wasn't going to be with Evelyn long though. Ronnie was telling me his lawyer was fighting hard to get her back and how much of a good chance they had. He also assured me that he had eyes on Evelyn place, watching out for Imani. I knew Ronnie would handle things and wouldn't let anything happen to our daughter, so that gave me some relief to know that Imani would be in good hands.

"Alright Ms. Robinson, you have some visitors today. Are you going to talk to them when they come?" the psychiatrist, Lois, said to me.

I was sitting in her office for my weekly session, doing the same thing I had been doing since I got here: not saying shit.

"Look Sky, I've been doing this a long time to know the difference between when a person is really crazy and when they just don't want to be bothered. You, my friend, are far from crazy. From reading over your files and talking to your fiancé and other people that know you, you have just been dealt a bad hand." Lois said.

I looked up at her when I heard her refer to Ronnie as my fiancé.

"I knew that would grab your attention." Lois smirked.

Feeling like she just got a slick one in, I quickly looked away from her and looked back out the window again.

"If you don't start showing these doctors that you don't need to be here, you're gonna get lost in the system Sky, and they're gonna keep pumping that medicine in you, which you don't want.," Lois expressed.

Every week she begged me to talk to her and show the doctors that I was sane, but I wasn't budging. "Fine, I'll notate your chart for the week and the nurse will come to get you for your visit with your guests." Lois let out a frustrated breath as she started writing in my chart.

Once she was done, she called for the nurse to come and get me. The nurse came in and we walked to the visiting room, where I took a seat, waiting for Ronnie. I'm sure Ms. Mary was coming with him as well since the psychiatrist said I had visitors coming today. Katrice hadn't come to see me since I've been here, but I don't blame her.

I loved when they came though, just so that I could see them and hear that they were doing okay. As I was sitting at the table, looking off into the direction opposite of the door, I heard footsteps coming my way.

"What's up baby?" I heard Ronnie's deep, sexy voice.

Turning my head in his direction, my heart stopped and tears formed in my eyes. There stood Ronnie holding Imani in his arms. My baby was reaching out for me when she saw me looking at her. Every thought that I had about my baby being better off without me subsided as I reached for her and grabbed her out of Ronnie's arms.

I cried so hard as I held onto Imani so tight.

I pulled her away from me and started checking over her body, looking at her arms, fingers, and legs.

"She's good Sky. You know I wouldn't let anything happen to my baby." Ronnie assured me as if he knew why I was checking her.

Knowing that she was with Evelyn caused me to panic. Relieved that I saw no bruises on Imani, I pulled her back into my chest and hugged my baby tight. I missed her so much!

Chapter Fifteen

KATRICE

I was now four months pregnant and my sickness still hadn't let up. The doctor told me that it should go away after three months, but that was a damn lie. I was trying my best to make this a mind over matter thing and enjoy my first pregnancy, but this shit was hard! Hearing my phone vibrate on the nightstand, I rolled over to grab it.

I saw that it was my mother calling me. I hit the ignore button and laid back down. Looking to my right, I noticed that Nick wasn't in our bed, which wasn't shocking. Since he and Ronnie decided to go legit, he's been busier now than when he was in the streets.

Nick had been investing and opening businesses, making sure his money flow kept building. Right now, he was dead set on opening his overnight daycare center, which I was so proud of him for doing so. I admit though, sometimes I find myself getting a little jealous of how my man is pushing forward in life and I'm just sitting here pregnant, not doing a damn thing.

This is not the chick I'm supposed to be. I stared up at the ceiling and let out a frustrated sigh. Things in my life were all fucked up right now. Since being home with too much time to think, my mind had been all over the place.

I missed Sky like crazy! Getting that call from Nick that day telling me that she was in the hospital for trying to kill herself almost caused me to lose my damn mind. The thought of not having her here on Earth with me any more scared me more than anything, especially when I still take blame for most of her recent pain she's endured. Although we haven't officially made up, I was still trying my best to be there for her.

I thanked God to this day for sparing her life when she tried slitting her wrist. Seeing her lying in that hospital bed like that was too much for me, so once I got confirmation that she was going to be okay, I stopped visiting her. Then when Nick told me that they had to put her in the mental hospital for a while, I wasn't going to go see her in that place.

I just couldn't bring myself to see her in a depressed state like that anymore. I knew she wasn't alone though, because Ronnie hadn't left her side once. Speaking of which, Ronnie had really been trying to fill his role as my big brother. He checked on me every day by calling, texting or just stopping by, and keeps me updated on Sky and Imani. I thought that it would be weird at first having him as a half-brother, but surprisingly, he fell right into the role perfectly.

Besides that, the only other sanity I had was Nick. The alert went off on my phone, indicating that I had a text message. Hoping that it was Nick, I reached back over to grab it and saw that my mother sent me a text asking me if I could come by the house this morning.

She was another one I didn't want to be around right now. All she did was cry about Damon and there was no way I could console her on that. Maybe it was my hormones, but I was secretly having mixed feelings about what happened to him. The empathetic side of me felt guilty because he was my brother, but the karma side said he got everything he deserved because of the horrible things he did to me, Celeste, Sky, and God knows who else.

Of course, I never expressed any of this to Nick; hell, I didn't even question if he had anything to do with Damon's death at all. This was really one of those don't ask, don't tell type of situations. Deep down, I knew that Nick and Ronnie handled Damon; shit, I knew that was coming after what he did to Sky, but I wasn't ready to hear it out loud and get confirmation just yet.

I looked over at the clock and noticed that it was after nine in the morning. Knowing that I wasn't about to go back to sleep, I got up and went to the bathroom to handle my morning hygiene. After throwing up from trying to brush my teeth, I was able to gargle and take a quick shower. Once I was done, I put on a pair of Nick's basketball shorts, a wife beater with no bra, and put my hair in a high ponytail.

Grabbing my phone off the nightstand, I headed downstairs to the kitchen to make me some toast. Hopefully, that'll help ease this morning sickness. While in the kitchen, waiting for my toast in the toaster oven, I leaned against the counter, contemplating if I should just go over to my mother's house today and get the shit over with.

I hadn't seen her since finding out that I was pregnant, so she didn't even know that she was about to have her first grandchild. I also needed to ask her some questions pertaining to my daddy, and inform her of what I found out from Ronnie about him. Hearing the timer go off on the toaster oven, I went over and grabbed my toast. Opening the refrigerator for some jelly and grabbing the orange juice as well, the doorbell rang.

Wondering who could be at my door, since no one knew where we lived now, but Ronnie, I went to answer the door. Looking through the peephole, I saw a short, red skinned chick standing there. Curious, I opened the door.

"Hi, can I help you?" I asked her.

She sized me up and down with a stank ass look plastered on her face and her hand on her hip. I knew this bitch was about to be on dumb shit, and I wasn't here for it.

"I'm here to see Nick." this bitch spoke, rolling her eyes and sucking her teeth.

"Nick isn't here, who can I tell him came by?" I asked, trying my best to stay calm and not knock the shit out this bitch.

"Yeah, tell him Kim came by; his baby momma." she smirked, rubbing her stomach.

Chapter Sixteen

ISIS

I was tired of dealing with the bullshit here in West Palm with Gerald. This nigga thought he was pimping my ass out, when in fact, I was the one playing him. For the past two weeks, I've been keeping in contact with Tracey, one of the dancers at the club back in Miami, trying to see if there was any word out about me and Gerald. So far, Tracey told me that ain't shit popping on the streets, and that she hadn't heard anything.

She would know too; this bitch was the fucking street Miami Herald newspaper. Her ass knew everybody's business and the latest tea. Hell, even the dope boys would go to her if they wanted to know if their shit was about to be raided or not. Once I knew things were clear for me to go back, that's when I put my plan in motion to leave Gerald's ass right up here.

I knew that it would piss him off that I left, and there was a possibility that his crazy ass might try and come after me, but fuck that. I'll cross that bridge when I get there. At first, I was all for riding this out with him and going to North Carolina. Shit, I wanted to be the top-notch bitch standing by his side when he took over those streets. He had the means to know how to do so since he already knew how the game went, but his muthafuckin ass had developed a coke habit.

When I first found his stash in the drawer of the night table, he told me that he only used it from time to time to help with the pain from being shot. I excused that, but then I started noticing how every time I would leave and come back, his ass would be laid out high with the shit on the table. Then, one day, when I left in the morning to go meet up with a trick, the motel manager stopped me in the parking lot and told me that we either had to pay him the back rent or get out.

Now, I know that I wasn't giving Gerald all the fucking money I made from tricking, but I did give his ass more than enough to pay for the damn room, which he claimed he was doing. I told the manager that I would pay him the money later that day, which I had no plans of doing. Later, when I got back to the room, Gerald's ass was high again. Right when I was about to tell his ass about me finding out how he wasn't paying for our room, he pulled his dick out and I got side tracked.

So far, all the men I was fucking for money were old heads, so I was glad when Gerald was up for giving me some of his good dick. While fucking, that nigga had the nerve to call me Sky's name when he came and then rolled over like it wasn't shit and went to sleep. I jumped in the shower for a quick wash up, grabbed all my shit quietly while he was still knocked out, and hauled ass.

I was on I-95 south, heading back to Miami now. Gerald had already called my phone five times since I had been driving. I guess his ass must have finally woken up, but fuck him. Sick of him blowing my shit up, I called T-Mobile and had them change my number. Now, I wouldn't have to worry about his ass for now.

Still driving, my mind wandered. Reaching for my phone in the passenger seat, I grabbed it and scrolled down my contacts to Ronnie's name. Smiling, I sent him a text: *HEY STRANGER.* I pressed send, hoping that he'd answer my message. Since Tracy told me that shit was clear back at home, I wasn't worried about if Ronnie knew about me having dealings with Gerald or not. Seconds later, my phone went off. I snatched it back up and smiled when I saw that Ronnie had texted me back.

FUTURE BAE: WHO THIS?

I was about to catch a serious attitude when he texted me that shit, but then quickly remembered that I had just changed my number.

ME: My bad, this is Ebony. I had to change my number.

I never gave Ronnie my first name, just in case Sky ever mentioned she had a sister named Isis. Instead, I gave him my middle name.

FUTURE BAE: Damn, you must have a lot of stalkers lol.

ME: Nope, just decided to have a fresh start with everything.

FUTURE BAE: Ain't nothing wrong with that, so what you been up to?

I got so excited from texting Ronnie that it was hard to concentrate on the road.

ME: Just working, getting this money and thinking about you. Wby? (what about you)

FUTURE BAE: Same thing this way, getting money and taking care of my daughter.

This was the first-time Ronnie ever mentioned he had a daughter to me. This made me wonder how things were with him and Sky right now. I still didn't know if she mentioned anything about me being with Gerald, but then again, Ronnie still didn't know that I was her sister.

ME: Well, that's what's up. I'm driving so when I get some time I'll hit you up and maybe we could do lunch.

FUTURE BAE: Alright, just hit me up.

As much as I didn't want our mini conversation to end, I got nervous when he mentioned his daughter. After about an hour of driving, because of the construction being done on the expressway, I finally pulled up to my momma's house. I cut my car off and hesitated before getting out. I already knew she was about to talk shit because I had been gone this long and left my kids with her, but fuck it. When I gave her this money I had, she'd shut the fuck up.

Chapter Seventeen

RONNIE

"*D*amn nigga, you all over there smiling in yo' phone and shit." Nick teased, cutting his eyes over at me.

We were in his low-key car, an all-black Impala, on the expressway, heading to West Palm Beach to finish this fuck nigga Gerald. I know his ass thought that he got away and we didn't know where the fuck he was at, but that was far from the truth. That day when we busted in his shit, we found his ass in the kitchen. Soon as I saw him, I started shooting.

I know I hit fool a couple of times. When he was down and not moving, I instructed Nick and the rest of the boys to go look for Sky. I don't know how, but suddenly, when I turned my attention back to Gerald, his ass was gone. We searched that house high and low for him but came up short.

It wasn't until I got Sky out of there that Ronnie found a

floorboard removed in another back room, which led under the house. Since it was an old house sitting on bricks, that made it easier to escape. His ass got away that day, but twenty-four hours later, I already had word on his where-abouts. His pussy ass went to the emergency room in West Palm Beach and had been hiding out at some raggedy ass motel up there since then.

He's so fucking dumb; he even reached out to one of the dope boys up there to bring him some fucking coke. Dumb ass mutha-fucka didn't even know old boy that was bringing it to him worked for me. Gerald thought he knew shit about me, but apparently, he didn't know how far my reach and pull was. I wasn't just known in Miami, I had all of Florida on lock, so there wasn't anywhere his ass could hide in my state that I wouldn't find him.

I'd been giving him some time to think that we didn't know where he was so that he could get comfortable and not see us coming. So, we were finally on our way to do this nigga in.

We heard he also had a bitch that was with him, so if her ass was there when we got there, her ass was just as dead as he was about to be. It was three a.m.; the perfect time to catch a body.

"I was just texting Ebony back." I responded to Nick.

"You still talking to lil mama from the club?"

"Every now and then. It's been a minute though and she just hit me up." I replied.

Nick's phone started ringing again. Since we had been

driving, his shit had been going off like every five minutes, but he kept ignoring it.

"Aye man, you good? Why you keep ignoring your phone?" I questioned.

"Yeah, I'm straight. Just some chicken head who I used to have dealings with that keeps trying to get at ya boy." Nick responded.

I didn't know whether he was telling the truth or not, but I was staying out his business on this. Ever since I found out that Katrice was my little sister, I had quickly developed an overprotective, big brother relationship with her. She was already cool with me before finding out that we were related. She and Nick were about to be a family and it seemed like their shit was solid, so I trusted him to know that he wouldn't do anything dumb to fuck up his home.

"Here go the exit right here." I heard Nick say as he switched over to the right lane to get off the expressway.

Ten minutes later, we pulled into the parking lot of the motel and parked across the street from it on the side of the road. Already dressed in black, Nick reached under his seat to grab our ski masks. Handing me mine, we both put our masks on and crept out the car; checking our surroundings, making sure no one saw us.

Pulling my silencer out from the front of my sweat pants, Nick nodded his head, giving me the okay that he was strapped and ready to go. We ran across the street, into the parking lot of the motel, and crept to the side of the building.

We already knew the security cameras that they had here didn't work, so we didn't have to worry about that.

Locating the room number that Gerald was in, we both stood on each side of the door. There was a glare that we saw from the curtains; I peeped in and saw that it was coming from the television. I took the copy key out of my pocket, courtesy of the dope boy who got it from the manager. The manager let him do business here, so as long as he broke him off some cash on the side, he was good.

Anyway, I put the key in the door and slowly opened it. Walking inside, we found this nigga sprawled on the bed in his boxers, mouth wide open, snoring. Closing the door quietly, we walked farther into the room. This shit smelled like straight ass mixed with funk. Walking closer to the bed, I saw a tray with coke left on it from Gerald doing some lines. Nick started checking the room out, making sure nobody else was in this bitch.

"Wake yo' ass up, nigga!" I screamed as I kicked his leg that was hanging off the bed.

"What the fuck, Isis? Where the fuck you been?" Gerald mumbled as he started to sit up.

You could tell that he was fucked up. Once he sat up, he adjusted his eyes and looked like he saw a ghost when he saw me standing there.

"Yeah muthafucka, thought you weren't gone see me so soon, huh?" I taunted as I pulled my gun from out of my waist and pointed it at his head.

Gerald scooted back to the headboard. You could tell he

was scared, but then suddenly, he dropped his shoulders and let out a deep breath. By his body language, I could tell that he knew this shit was over for him.

"Man, do what the fuck you came here to do." was all he said.

I didn't hesitate to pull the trigger twice, shooting him once in the head, and once in the chest. Gerald's body slumped over as blood began to pour out of his body. Normally, I would call the clean-up crew to come and handle this mess but decided to leave this nigga here. Nick gave the okay that the room was clear.

"Snake ass, junky bitch. Let's roll." I said to Nick as I headed towards the door to leave.

Back outside, we jogged back to the car and pulled off. Not saying a word, Nick reached in his ashtray and pulled out a blunt. I already knew what time it was, so I laid back and took a pull as he passed it to me. Now that I got that fuck nigga Gerald out the way for good this time, I concentrated on getting my family back in order.

I had been blowing up Katrice's phone for the past two days, and her ass still wasn't picking up for me. Her voicemail was full and I'm sure it was because of me leaving her voicemail after voicemail. I fucked up big time and I didn't know how the fuck I was going to get myself out of this situation. Kim's stupid ass showed up at my crib and told Katrice that I got her ass pregnant; I don't even know how her ass knew where we stayed.

No one knew I was fucking with Kim, not even Ronnie. After Ronnie had warned me about her that day, I had every intention of leaving her ass alone, but that bitch had some bomb pussy and head. At that time, I wasn't committed to anyone, so I decided to still fuck with her ass from time to time on some low-key type shit. When things became official with Katrice and me, I ended shit with me and Kim.

At first, Kim wasn't taking no for an answer, and would call crying, begging and shit, but I kept ignoring her. Then when Katrice called me that day telling me that she wanted to come to my crib because she and her momma got into it, I was at Kim's crib, trying to let her ass know that shit was done between me and her.

Kim was on some dramatic shit, crying and telling me how she loved a nigga. How the fuck you love me when the only time I came around was to fuck and get some head? I never took her ass on a date or was seen with her out in public. She was a stripper hoe who let me fuck her ass the first night we met in the parking lot in my car.

There was no way I was wifing her ass up. In the midst of her begging me that day, my dick somehow ended up in her mouth. After I came all down her throat, I left out her shit that day and headed home to my woman. Kim kept calling me afterward, but after two weeks of me straight ignoring her, I figured she got the picture and moved the fuck on.

Then, two months later, out the blue, I get a text from her telling me that she was pregnant. My initial thought was to text her ass back and tell her to go find her real baby daddy because it wasn't me, but then I remembered that there could be a possibility that if she was indeed pregnant, that could be my jit. I slipped up a couple of times with Kim and didn't use a condom; some in-the-heat-of-the-moment bullshit where I figured I'd just pull out.

So, I sent her a text back telling her that I would come through her crib *later* that night. When I got there, that's when Kim told me that she was about two months along. All I heard was that it still wasn't too late for her ass to get an abortion.

"Aye man, I ain't trying to have no baby or no baby momma right now. You need to handle that." I said to her as I took a roll out of my pocket and peeled off fifteen hundred dollars, tossing it on the kitchen table.

I knew that was more than enough for her to have an abortion, but I gave her extra just to shut her ass up.

"Really Nick? So, you just gone nut all up in me, get me pregnant and then think shit all good by giving me money to get a fucking abortion!" she yelled.

"Check this out Kim. Truthfully, you ain't nobody for me to debating with, ma. I told you this shit time and time again; it wasn't nothing but a fuck thing with us. I never told you that you were my bitch, I never took you out, I never showed face with you in public, and I never even took you to my crib. When I wanted some pussy, I called and you answered; that's it. Ain't no way in hell I'm about to have a baby with *yo' ass, so take that money and handle that.*"

She started cursing and going off, calling me all types of fuck niggas, but that shit didn't faze me. I left her place and went home to dick Katrice down. I thought Kim had finally come to her senses when I didn't hear anything else from her; that was until I got home the other day and Katrice went in on my ass.

Soon as she told me that Kim came to the house and said

that she was pregnant with my baby, I knew I couldn't lie about the shit. Truth was, I loved Katrice and hated like hell that I hurt her this way, especially when was she carrying my seed. I ended up confessing everything to her, but also made it clear that when I first found out about Kim being pregnant that I gave her money for an abortion, so I didn't know that she was still pregnant.

Seeing Katrice break down and cry that day cut me to the core. I wanted to choke the shit out of Kim's stupid ass for showing up to my shit. Katrice left out that day, saying she needed some time to think, but that was two days ago and her ass still hadn't been back home.

Kim, on the other hand, had been calling and texting me nonstop. That's who was blowing my phone up the other night when I was in the car with Ronnie, but I had yet to talk to this bitch. I already knew her slimy ass took the money I gave her for the abortion and spent it, so right now, there wasn't shit that she could tell me.

Calling Katrice's phone again, I threw my phone back down on the couch when her voicemail came on saying that it was full.

"Fuck!" I screamed out.

Shit wasn't supposed to be like this. I fucked up big time and now I could have two babies on the way, at the same time, by two different women. One I want to spend the rest of my life with, and the other, I could give a fuck about. *Fuck this shit,* I thought to myself as I picked my phone back up.

Chapter Nineteen

SKY

$\mathcal{I}$t's been two weeks since I've been home, and I feel like I'm still in the mental hospital. After Ronnie brought Imani to see me, I knew I had to dig deep and get myself together. Seeing my baby lit a spark in me, so after a month in that place, the doctors finally agreed that I was sane enough to go home and not hurt myself.

That day, when I was released, Ronnie, Imani, and Ms. Mary were all there waiting for me, ready to take me home. Since I've been home, Ronnie and Ms. Mary had been hovering over me as if they were the fucking counselors at the hospital. I was on eggshells at home. I felt like my every move was being watched by them, but what hurt the most was I feel like they won't allow me to be alone with Imani.

There was still a lot of unanswered questions and things that weren't being discussed between Ronnie and I. Like what happened to Gerald or Damon since he told me that I wouldn't have to worry about them anymore. He also told me that he found out that he and Katrice were half brother and sister, which made Damon his damn brother. That shit really threw me for a loop, but he didn't go into the details and I hadn't asked for them either. Let's not forget the fact that I still hadn't heard anything from Isis.

"Bae, Nick is about to come over. He needs to discuss some shit with me, so I'll be in my office with him for a while." I looked up to Ronnie standing in the doorway of the bathroom.

I had just finished getting out the shower and was standing in the mirror with my towel wrapped around me. This was the closest Ronnie had gotten to see me almost naked in a while, so I was self-conscious. Even though I told Tracey, the psychiatrist at the mental health facility, that I was ready to take things slow and let Ronnie in again, I wasn't so sure.

Don't get me wrong, I loved him and all that he had done for me and our daughter, but deep down, I felt that I was more of a burden to him. Since first meeting Ronnie, he had always been there, cleaning up my shit and trying to get me to do better. Look what happens every time I try and do things on my own; I fuck things up and then Ronnie has to clean up behind me.

Then there's the intimate part of us. I'm pretty sure there's no way in hell that he wants to touch me like that again; why would he? I've been so violated by other men, resulting in me catching an STD, having tearing in my ass, and needing stitches to sew me back together.

I was so fucking damaged inside and out that certainly, Ronnie wished he could be elsewhere, instead of standing here looking at me in my bathrobe. Turning to look at him, I noticed how quickly he turned his head from looking in my direction.

"Well, that's fine. I thought that I could spend some time with Imani today anyway." I said to him.

It was Saturday and I wanted to put every negative thought that I had out of my mind and enjoy my daughter.

"That's good. You two should order some pizza and watch some movies. She definitely loves that *Frozen* shit; I swear I watched it so much I can hear the damn songs in my sleep." Ronnie joked, laughing.

I smiled. It felt good to hear him speak of Imani with so much love like a father should. In the short time that he'd been in her life, he already knew her like the back of his hand, and she had him wrapped around hers.

"Okay, we'll do that." I stuttered, not making eye contact.

"I'll be in my office if you need me." Ronnie turned and left out the room.

I turned around and looked at myself in the mirror, and I didn't recognize the woman staring back at me. My face was sunken in due to the weight I had lost from not eating, I had dark circles around my eyes, my hair was in two big braids going back with my baby hairs sticking up, and my face broke out terribly with acne. I turned on the water in the sink, closed the door, and started crying, hoping the water would drown out the sound.

How could my life come to this? Right now, I should be in college with Katrice, having Imani with me, and getting an education so that I could provide a better life for her. I stood there crying for a few seconds, then splashed water on my face. Drying my face off with a hand towel, I applied some moisturizer on my face and put Chap Stick on my lips.

Taking down the two braids, I let my hair loose, displaying it's naturally curly texture.

I went inside the bedroom and lotioned myself up with my Victoria's Secret Angel body cream and spray, then I put on my PINK tights and matching cami. I tried my best to look better than I felt. Looking myself over in the full-length mirror, I took a deep breath and went downstairs.

"Now, don't you look refreshing and cute! Come on in here so I can put some meat on them bones." Ms. Mary greeted me as I walked into the kitchen.

Ms. Mary was standing over the stove, stirring what looked to be a pot of grits. Imani was in her high chair, eating, making a mess with the bacon and eggs in front of her. I walked over to my baby and gave her a kiss on her fat little cheeks, which caused her to laugh.

"Good morning Ms. Mary." I spoke as I took a seat at the island.

"Morning baby, how you feeling?" she asked.

"I'm feeling fine." I responded with a faint smile.

"Um-huh, the sooner you are truthful with yourself, the better you'll be." Ms. Mary turned around, looking at me.

I already knew there was no fooling her, and personally, I was tired of putting on this damn show. Right when I was about to open up and let Ms. Mary know the truth, the door-bell rang.

"I'll get that." I got up from the bar stool and went to see who was at the front door.

Looking at the surveillance camera we had on the hallway table, I saw that it was Nick standing at the front door. I walked over to the door and let him in.

"How you doing lil sis? You looking good." Nick said as he gave me a hug.

"Thanks, bruh." I replied, stepping aside so that he could come inside.

"How's Katrice?" I asked Nick.

"She good." he answered quickly.

I could tell by his body language and the way he avoided eye contact with me that something wasn't right. I hadn't spoken to Katrice since kicking her out of my house the day she confessed those things to me about Damon, so I'm pretty sure I've been missing out on a lot. Deciding not to press the issue with Nick, I told him that Ronnie was upstairs in his office.

"Ms. Mary, I'll be right back!" I yelled out as I walked passed the kitchen and went back upstairs to the bedroom and grabbed my phone off the dresser.

Unlocking it, I went to my contacts until I got to Katrice's name and sent her a text message saying that I wanted to meet up. Thank God all my contacts were imported over to the new phone Ronnie got me. Seconds later, Katrice texted me back saying that she missed me and couldn't wait to meet up. We agreed that she would come over to the house this afternoon so that we could talk.

I left out the part about Nick already being over here though, because I didn't want to risk the chance of her not coming. A blind person could see by the reaction Nick gave me earlier that shit wasn't right between him and Katrice, and right now, I think my best friend and I needed one another.

Chapter Twenty

KIM

"Stupid ass nigga!" I threw my phone on the floor when Nick's fuck ass sent me to the voicemail again.

I knew he was salty because I popped up at his house and told his bitch that I was pregnant, but fuck that! Her ass wasn't about to be the only one walking around here trying to bag his ass. Everyone knew that Nick was the next big thing to Ronnie, and since I couldn't get to Ronnie, thanks to Sky's ass, I wasn't about to lose out on Nick. I had always been the type of bitch that went after what she wanted and didn't give a damn about who got fucked up in the process.

Growing up, I watched my momma use niggas and get whatever she could out of their asses. She always told me that if you thought with your heart and not with your pussy, you would always get fucked over; not fucked.

We always had more of a sister relationship, than a mother-daughter relationship. So, anything I did or didn't do, that was on me, with her not giving a damn. Whether I decided to go to school or not, stay out as late as I wanted, smoke or drink, my momma couldn't care less. That's how I knew how to get money at an early age, so when Sky first approached all of us back then with the idea to not fuck with dudes unless they were paying us, I was already steps ahead of the bitch.

Sky always thought that she was better than the rest of us, when her ass was sucking and fucking just like we were. But I guess she called herself turning over a new leaf and left us hanging when she got with Ronnie. She knew how much I was feeling him. I used to always talk about how fine he was and how I wanted to fuck him. I even tried throwing the pussy at him on the sly, but he never took the bait.

But as soon as I looked up, her ass was the one that had to have him. Most would say that I was hating, but I didn't hate on Sky; I hated Sky. She always thought that she was the top-notch bitch in the group, the one that didn't need the weave like the rest of us, and refused to talk to the same niggas we dealt with. Then when she got with Ronnie, she stopped hanging out with us all together.

Word was that he didn't want her to roll with us anymore, but what type of weak bitch would allow a nigga to tell her who she can and can't hang out with? When Ronnie got knocked off and went to jail, I thrived off seeing Sky walk around all depressed and shit. Our other homegirls were the ones feeling sorry for her, but not me.

That's why when I saw Gerald taking her pussy, Instead of helping her, I just stood there and enjoyed the view. Prior to that, Sky called herself trying to shine on my ass in front of folks at a block party we were at. When I noticed that she saw me looking at her and Gerald, I smiled and hauled ass, leaving him to finish up.

Later that night, I came up with the plan to write Ronnie in jail and tell him how I caught Gerald and Sky fucking, and how I would always see Gerald coming out of her place. I also included my number on the letter, telling him to call me. After I had sent the letter off, I waited by the phone and mailbox for a fucking month, waiting on this nigga to call, but I never heard shit from him. Then, Sky's grandma died and she moved away to live with her momma.

I tried keeping tabs on the bitch, just to see if she was miserable or not, but she switched to a different school and stopped taking everyone's calls. Since no one knew where her momma stayed, she just stayed ghost. After that, I ended up hooking up with Gerald, only to have his ass always asking me about Sky, so I left him alone. Once I turned seventeen, I was able to get a job at Coco's Strip Club, since I fucked with the owner from time to time, and really make some money.

I ended up dropping out of school, since I barely went anyway, and moved out on my own into the projects for about a year. I just had one of these older chicks I knew sign off on a lease for me since I was still under age. After a while, I made enough money to move into a better apartment in the North Miami Beach area. It was no secret that I did more than shaking my ass for money. Shit, I had no problems throwing my pussy to the highest bidder.

Imagine my luck when I was at work one night and saw Ronnie and Nick walk through. My initial plan was to finally be able to have a go at Ronnie. Although he never responded to my letter or called me, I surely wasn't the young bitch he knew from back in the days, and I was ready to show him just that.

When Ronnie saw me, his look alone already told me that he didn't want to be fucked with, so I directed my attention over to Nick. That night, we fucked in the parking lot of the club, and had been fucking since then; well, up until a few months ago.

I'm not stupid. It was obvious Nick had a bitch at home. I mean, let's be real; the nigga never did take me out or took me to his crib. Hell, the only reason I knew where he stayed was because one day I saw him and his chick in Walmart while I was in there getting a few things. I secretly followed them until they left out the store, and then tailgated their asses all the way to their house.

Nick never even gave me the indication that he wanted to be my nigga, but I did something with him that I had never done before with any other dude; I let my heart do the talking this time. Don't get me wrong, the dick was good, but Nick had the whole package and I wanted it!

He was fine as hell; his body was built like a God covered

with tattoos all down his caramel skin, and he had lips that would put LL Cool J to shame. I tried countless times to get him to touch me with those lips, but he refused every time. Oh, and let's not forget how long his money was. That's why when I found out that I was pregnant, I just knew his ass would be stuck with me.

Of course, he gave me the bullshit ass story about not wanting to have a baby and threw me a little over a stack to get rid of it, but he had me fucked up if he thought I was about to have my meal ticket sucked out of me. That's why I waited until I was showing and it would be too late for me to have an abortion to do a pop up on his ass at his house.

It did fuck my head up though when his hoe answered the door and I saw that she was pregnant as well. So, I politely told her ass to let Nick know that his baby momma Kim came by, and left. That had been almost a week ago and I still hadn't heard anything from him.

"That nigga still not answering yo' calls?" Charlene asked me as she blew out smoke from her blunt.

Charlene was another dancer at the club, and we kicked it from time to time with having a smoke and drinking session. I stopped fucking with the chicks who I used to roll with, and occasionally kicked it with some of the girls from the club. We all seemed to have more in common and could relate to one another better. Right now, I was chilling at her place, getting fucked up on this good ass weed.

Shit, I didn't give a damn if I was pregnant or not; no baby was about to stop me from living my fucking life. I wanted

Nick and if I had to sacrifice my body for nine months for this lil muthafucka to make it into the world, then so be it.

"Hell no. Girl, I'm about to take that drive and do a drive by on his ass, though." I admitted.

I was tired of playing these games with Nick. If he thought that he was going to walk around here and only claim that bitch's baby, he had me fucked up! True enough, there was a strong possibility that this baby might not be his, but shit, he didn't know that. So, for now, he's my baby daddy just as much as his hers.

"Bitch, you tripping. Didn't you say his ass stayed out there in Weston somewhere? If he ain't answering yo' calls, what makes you think he's gone answer his door?" Charlene questioned me, shaking her head.

"I don't give a fuck Charlene. That nigga ain't about to play me for no other bitch, especially when I'm pregnant with his baby too!" I said, getting pissed off.

"Allegedly!" Charlene blurted out laughing.

I didn't find shit funny. Now I wish that I wouldn't have ever told this bitch that this baby might not be Nick's.

"Whatever. Like I said, he's not about to keep fucking trying me." I waved her off.

"See, I thought you had more common sense than this." Charlene said, passing me the blunt.

"What you talking about?" I cut my eyes over at her as I took a pull.

"You already know how this shit goes, girl. That nigga ain't leaving his bitch for no stripper hoe." Charlene replied to me.

"A stripper hoe?" I turned my head to her, ready to pop off if I had to.

"Don't catch an attitude with me for keeping it one hundred with you. You already know how these niggas think, and believe me, Nick's ass ain't no different. You wanna play this shit out, then you gotta be smart. All this popping up to his crib and calling and texting ain't gone get you shit but what it's doing now, and that's ignored." Charlene explained.

"So, tell me how the fuck I'm supposed to get his attention then? I know his bitch already told him that I came by their house and that I was pregnant too."

"First off, you need to be smart about this. You wanna trap this nigga into thinking that this is his baby? Then don't be the thirsty, desperate bitch. Go at his ass calm, cool, and collected; something he won't expect. Play the nice, no drama chick who just wants to co-parent. Trust me when I say his chick wouldn't be able to stand that shit. They'll start beefing in their household and you'll start to be his safety net. You gotta think smart, bitch, not act off yo' emotions."

I sat back, higher than a muthafucka, but still lucid enough to grasp everything Charlene had just said to me. She was right though. I did need to calm down and play this shit right, especially if I wanted my man and wanted us to be a family.

Chapter Twenty-One

KATRICE

The last place I wanted to be was back at my mom's place, but I couldn't be around Nick right now. When that bitch, Kim, showed up to our house and said that she was pregnant by Nick, my heart stopped. I know that we haven't been together for a long time, but as far as I knew, I was the only woman walking around here carrying his seed.

Before I had a chance to respond to what she had just told me, the bitch hauled ass back to her car and sped out of our driveway. I just stood in the doorway for a few minutes, trying to wrap my mind around what the fuck just happened. I was so confused and had too many questions that I needed to be answered right at that fucking moment.

I ran back inside and called Nick. After the second ring, he answered the phone, sounding like he didn't have a care in the fucking world.

"What's up beautiful?" Nick answered.

"Nick, I need you to get your ass home, now!" I yelled into the phone and hung up before he could respond.

He tried calling me back twice, but I didn't answer. What I wanted to know and say needed to be done face to face. I sat down on the living room couch, shaking my leg, as I waited for Nick's ass to walk through the door. About thirty minutes later, I heard the chirping from the alarm, indicating that the front door opened.

"Katrice, what's wrong? You okay?" Nick rushed into the living room, in a panic.

"I'mma ask you this one time, so be careful on how you answer me; who the fuck is Kim?" I threw at him.

I looked this nigga right in his face, praying that he would tell me the truth. I would hate to have to catch a case if his ass decided to lie to me.

Nick stood there for a while as if he was contemplating on what he was about to say. He walked over to where I was sitting on the couch, and took a seat next to me.

"Alright bae, I'm not gone lie to you. Kim is a bitch who works at Coco's that I used to fuck with from time to time." he began to explain.

"Was this before us or during?" I asked.

My heart started pounding so loud that I thought it was about to jump out my chest. I was so afraid of what he was about to say next.

"It was before us, and once during us." he admitted, putting his head down.

I wanted to cry so badly, but I refused to let this nigga see tears come from me.

"So, what you're sitting here telling me is that not only did you cheat on me with this bitch, but you also got us both pregnant at the same time?" I screamed out.

I may not have been crying, but that didn't mean I wasn't about to let his ass have it!

"Pregnant?" Nick looked at me confused.

"Yeah nigga, pregnant! That bitch showed up here today with her big ass stomach telling me to tell yo' stupid ass that she came by!" I yelled as I nudged him in the side of his head.

"Look Katrice, I know you pissed, but you really need to keep your hands to yourself." Nick said as he turned to face me. "Now, as far as her being pregnant, I didn't know that."

"Did you fuck her without a condom?" I asked him.

By the hesitance I saw on his face, I already knew what he was about to say. "I slipped up once." He confessed again.

"Then that's all it takes, dummy!" I jumped up.

"I can't believe this shit, man! Every time I try and give a nigga a chance, he always does me wrong! You ain't no better than my ex!" This time, I couldn't hold my tears back as they started coming down my face.

"Don't put me in the category of that nigga. I fucked up, but I ain't running from shit; I'm owning up to it. I didn't know Kim was pregnant, Katrice." Nick stood up and came close to me.

He tried to touch me, but I pulled away from him. Whether he knew she was pregnant or not, the fact remained that he cheated on me with the bitch, and me and her were both pregnant. Seeing how her ass just showed up to the house, I already knew she was about to be with drama, and right now, I wasn't up for it.

"I need some time to think." I said as I backed away from Nick and left out the living room.

"Where you going?" Nick questioned as he followed me into the kitchen, where I grabbed my purse and keys off the table.

"I need some air, Nick." I answered as I pushed past him and left out the front door.

The only place I knew I could go at the time was my mom's house, so here I was. Nick had been calling and texting me constantly, but I still wasn't ready to talk to his ass.

"Katrice, you need to eat something, baby." my mother said, barging into my old room.

When I showed back up on my mother's doorsteps with my belly, she immediately started crying. She was so happy at the thought of finally being a grandmother. She started throwing all types of questions at me about where I had been staying and who my baby's father was. At the time, I told her that I didn't feel like answering any questions and just wanted to rest. She left me alone for about a day, but after that, she was back to being fucking nosey and it was really working my nerves!

"Ma, can't you knock?" I said, irritated as I looked up at her.

I was lying down, trying to relax so that this nausea would go away.

"I can, but I didn't. It's time we talk, Katrice. You've been here long enough and I gave you your space like you asked, but enough is enough." My mom began as she came all the way inside of the room and sat at the desk.

Not wanting to, I sat up in the bed with my arms folded.

"Ever since I told you that your brother was found dead, you've been so distant. What kind of sister doesn't even show up to her own brother's funeral?" My mother called herself chastising me, but what she did was just piss me the hell off instead.

"You wanna know the kind of sister that doesn't show up to her brother's funeral? The kind of sister whose brother would come into her room at night and fuck her or make her suck his dick! The kind of sister who sat back and watched her brother do unforgivable things to other people, and the kind of sister who knew that her brother was an evil, lying manipulator! You always seemed to turn the blind eye when it came to Damon and Daddy, momma, but answer this for me---- How come you never believed me when I told you that Damon did all those things to me? How come his word was always better than mine?" I asked, now crying.

I could tell my mother wasn't expecting me to say all that by the look on her face. She put her head down in her hands and began to cry as well. The last thing I wanted to do was hurt my mother, but I was also tired of being hurt.

"I met my other brother from Daddy." I spoke out again.

My mom shot her head up and looked at me.

"How?" she asked.

Funny how she can ask me this, but couldn't say shit about all the other things I had just said. I shook my head, laughing.

"Does it matter? Daddy had another family, which I'm sure you were perfectly aware of, and I met him." I told her.

"Katrice, I know that you're angry at me, but things weren't that simple. It wasn't that I didn't believe you, baby, but Damon wasn't that type of boy." She cried out, still defending Damon.

"Do you hear yourself Ma? You think I would lie about something like that!"

"Katrice, you got pregnant at an early age and had an abortion; ain't no telling what the hell you would do!" she yelled, throwing up my past in my face.

I couldn't believe she had just said that shit out of her mouth. We never mentioned that up until now. I had never in my life wanted to disrespect my mother, but after today, it would be a very long time before she saw me again. Sky texted me earlier, which I was glad about, and asked me to come over to her place later this afternoon so we could talk, but I was about to leave and go over there sooner than expected.

Not saying anything, I got out of the bed, walked over to the closet and grabbed my shoes and purse. Putting on my shoes, I turned around to address my mother one last time before leaving out.

"You know what, Ma, I love you and always will. You clothed me, took care of me, and were there for me most of the times, but not when I needed you the most. It hurts to know that you took the time to *think* that you knew your son." I emphasized that word. "but not me. I wish you nothing but the best mommy, but until you can be truthful with me and own up to the shit that was done, not only have you lost a son, but you just lost a daughter and possibly a grandchild." With that said, I kissed my mom on the cheek and left out of her house, and possibly her life.

Chapter Twenty-Two

RONNIE

I sat back in my chair and tried to digest everything Nick had just said to me. I couldn't believe the shit that was coming out of his mouth.

"So you mean to tell me that, even after I warned you about the hoe, telling you not to fuck with her, you did it anyway? Now her ass walking around here saying she's pregnant with your seed, the same time as Katrice?" I reiterated to him what he just told me.

"Yeah man. I fucked up big time with Katrice, dog." Nick sighed as he rubbed his hands down his face.

I already knew his ass was more than stressed the fuck out. Shit, it ain't even my situation and I'm stressing with him.

"Losing Katrice? Nigga, if that hoe Kim is pregnant by you, which the bitch is probably lying about anyway, you fucked for the rest of these eighteen years! Look man, you already know you fucked up big time, so I'm not about to keep reminding you of the shit. What's done is done; the next step is seeing how you gone handle all this." I reached inside my top desk drawer and pulled out a blunt from my stash.

From the shit Nick just threw out there, we both needed to be high right now. I lit the blunt, took a few pulls, and handed it across the desk to Nick.

"I already know that hoe Kim is trying to use me for a meal ticket, so the plan is to only see her when the shorty born so that I can get a DNA." Nick explained. "As far as Katrice, man, that's home. I refuse to lose her and my baby over that hoe Kim, so she's bringing her ass home; I do need you to talk to her for me, though."

"Talk to her? What you want me to say?" I asked.

"Shit man, I don't know! That's your sister, but I'm your brother. I didn't mean for this shit to happen; That's why I gave Kim's stupid ass money to get an abortion when she first came to me with this pregnancy shit. Far as I was concerned, she took care of that." Nick shook his head as he pulled from the blunt again.

"That's where you fucked up at again. You were supposed to take her ass to the clinic and make sure the shit got done, not just give her ass the money. The bitch a stripper hoe and fucked you in the parking lot, in a car the first night she met you; what else you thought she was gone do with the fucking money? That hoe probably spent that shit on those raggedy ass bundles of weave she be having in her hair." I laughed.

Nick looked at me pissed, but I didn't give a fuck. Shit, this was his doing, so he was going to have to ride this out the best way he could. Of course, I was going to help my boy out, but I wasn't about to involve myself in him and Katrice's business. He was right; she was my sister and I loved her as such, but they were grown.

"Alright, I'll put a bug in lil sis' ear, but the hard work is on you man." I assured him.

"Bet, thanks, man. I'mma make this shit right. Katrice's ass ain't been answering my calls or texts, and her ass ain't been home."

"Where the fuck you think she at?" I questioned as he passed the blunt back to me.

"I rode by her moms' house yesterday and saw her car parked in the driveway, so she's been there. I almost got out my shit and went to knock on the door, but I figured I'd give her a little space. But shit, while Katrice's ass ignoring me, Kim won't stop calling me!" Nick blew out a long frustrated breath.

"I know you said that you didn't wanna talk to her until the baby was born, but maybe you need to holler at her beforehand and see where the fuck her head at. If you gone handle this shit, you gotta take care of it from all angles." I explained.

Nick and I sat there for the next thirty minutes or so, talking over shit. By the time we were done, we were both high, mellow, and hungry as fuck. I remembered Sky agreeing earlier to ordering some pizza for her and Imani, so we got up and headed downstairs to see if she had ordered the pizza because we both had the munchies. As we headed down the stairs, we heard the voices of different people talking. I know I wasn't expecting any fucking company in my house, so I was curious as to who the fuck was over here.

Nick and I walked into the living room to see Sky, Imani, Ms. Mary, and Katrice all sitting around, talking. Katrice was sitting in the middle of the living room floor, in Indian style, with Imani on her lap. Soon as me and Nick stepped in the room, all the talking stopped and all eyes were on us.

"Damn, don't stop talking just because we came down here." I joked as I walked over to the couch and took a seat next to Sky, wrapping my arm around her shoulder.

"Boy, watch your mouth, ain't nobody thinking about y'all." Ms. Mary said as she stood up from the loveseat she was sitting on and went to pick Imani up from Katrice's lap. "I'm about to put this one down for a nap, then I'll be back down to cook some shrimp gumbo for lunch. I hope *all y'all* are here to eat when I'm done cooking." Ms. Mary said as she looked around the room at her.

I already knew what she was hinting at, and I'm pretty sure everyone else did too. Ms. Mary left out the room with Imani in her arms, leaving the four of us downstairs. The room was so damn quiet that you could hear a rat piss on these marble floors.

"So, what's up, sis, you good?" I asked, directing my attention to Katrice.

"Humph, I'm pretty sure you already know the answer to

that." Katrice looked over at Ronnie, who was still standing up and rolled her eyes.

I wasn't about to try and talk to her in front of everyone, so I looked over at Ronnie as well, hoping he would start saying something his damn self. This was the first time that I saw my boy nervous. With shit still being awkward, I turned to Sky and kissed her on her right cheek.

"What about you, you good?" I said to her, looking in her eyes.

"I'm fine." Sky replied as she smiled at me.

Right when I was about to say something else, my phone started vibrating in my pocket. Pulling it out, I saw that it was Rob calling me.

"What's up, Rob?" I answered.

"Aye man, one of the houses been hit." He said on the other end of the phone.

"Come on man, you know that's all on you now." I replied.

The whole purpose of Nick and I getting out of the game and turning everything over to Rob was because we knew he would be able to handle this shit. So, there was no reason he should be calling me just because the trap houses got busted. I warned him beforehand that niggas were gone test his gangsta once they knew he was in charge now.

"It ain't just about the spot, Ronnie. Muthafucka left a message here with yo' name on it." I heard Rob say.

"Me and Nick about to swing through; where y'all at?"

"In the city." Rob answered.

I hung up the phone and looked up at Nick, who was already heading towards the front door.

"Bae, I gotta go handle some shit really quick, but when we come back, I want you and Katrice still here." I said to Sky as I kissed her on the lips and stood up to leave.

Before any questions could be asked by the girls, Nick and I were out the door and jumping into his truck.

"What Rob talking about?" Nick asked me as he cranked up his truck.

"He called to tell me that the trap house in the city got knocked off, and whoever did it left a message for me." I explained.

"Say no more." Nick put his truck in drive and pulled off, heading in the direction of the expressway.

I sat back in the passenger seat and closed my eyes to clear my head. I may have been out of the game, but I still had no problem showing muthafuckas that I was not the one to be fucked with.

Chapter Twenty-Three

ISIS

I've been back in Miami now for three weeks, and I was ready to leave this shit again; this time, not looking back. Besides my momma's begging ass constantly being in my damn ear about money, my kids were also getting on my damn nerves. The only peace I had was when I went to work at the club. Although I was gone for a while, I didn't have a problem getting my job back and picking up right where I left off.

"Girl, it's dead as fuck out there." One of the dancers, Charlene, said as she came in the locker room.

I had just got here about an hour ago, and when I walked in, I saw that it was slow. It was Friday and still early, though.

"That shit was buzzard when I walked in." I said to her as I opened my duffle bag and started taking out my costume for tonight.

When I first came into the locker room, it was quiet, so I decided to take a quick nap. Now that Charlene was back here; I already knew her ass was about to start gossiping about some other bitch's business. Charlene was what you would call a veteran around here. She was damn near thirty-five, but this bitch had the body that would put these young hoes to shame.

She only stripped here two nights out the week, and then headlined over at another big strip club, King of Diamonds. Charlene was a bad bitch indeed and stayed on her grind, but the bitch was as messy as they come. That hoe would pump you for information, let you cry on her shoulder, and then five minutes later, post about your ass on Facebook.

Just like I do these other hoes; I deal with her ass from a distance.

"So, bitch, where you been hiding at? I ain't see you around here for a minute; you must have snatched you up a paid nigga." Charlene asked me, being nosey.

See the shit I'm talking about? Her ass was always trying to find out shit, but she was barking up the wrong tree if she thought I was about to sit here and have a pow wow with her, telling her my business.

"I've just been chilling, girl, spending time with my kids." I lied as I pulled out my black diamond studded bikini bottom and matching top.

"Um-huh, but girl, yo' ass been missing all the tea going on over here!" Charlene got excited as she came over to where I was and got comfortable.

Here we go I thought to myself.

I sat there for the next fifteen minutes and listened to Charlene as she gave me the rundown on whose man which hoe was fucking, which dude came up here beating some nigga's ass over their chick and so on. By the time she was done giving me the rundown on everything, I felt like I had just read some shit off The Shaderoom on Instagram!

"Child, from everything you just told me, it sounds like I ain't miss shit. Same old shit, different day." I shrugged her off as I turned towards the mirror and started taking the flexi-rods out of my hair. Tonight, I felt like going for an exotic look. I knew the niggas would be rolling in later and I had plans to be deep in their pockets.

"Oh, I know you heard about your boy, Gerald." I heard Charlene say from behind me.

The mention of his name caused me to stop taking down my hair in mid-air and turn my attention to her.

"What happened?" I questioned, hoping she wasn't about to say that his ass was back in town and looking for me.

"Girl, that nigga was found dead in a motel in West Palm Beach!" she exposed.

I let out a short sigh of relief, hoping Charlene didn't notice that shit.

"Wait, what? When the fuck did this happen?" I was trying to act shocked, but I just needed to know if I was fully in the clear or not.

"All I heard was that he crossed some niggas and they

went and got his ass. Word was he was hiding up in West Palm, coked up." Charlene explained.

"Damn, that's fucked up. They know who did it?"

"If they do, they not saying. The news saying that the hotel manager believes it was just another crack head owing somebody some money. You already know the police ain't looking for nobody; to them, it's just another nigga off the streets." Charlene grabbed her back and left out the locker room, letting me know that she'd see me later.

I sat there stunned. A part of me was relieved that Gerald's ass was dead because I didn't have to worry about him fucking with me anymore. Something in my gut was telling me that Ronnie had a hand in this, and if that was true, then I needed to find out if he knew that I had any ties to Gerald. The only way I would know if I was in the clear was if I talked to Sky. I continued to sit there, contemplating on how I was going to approach her. I still hadn't heard from her since the accident and I wasn't sure if she thought that I was in on it.

Stuffing my outfit back into my duffle bag, I grabbed my purse and walked outside of the club to my car in the parking lot. Reaching my car, I unlocked the doors and got inside. Pulling my cell phone out from my purse, I scrolled down in my contacts until I reached Sky's name and took a deep breath.

I needed to know what she knew, and the only way I could get that information would be to hear it from her myself; that's why I came outside to my car so that I could have some peace and quiet while I made this overdue phone call. Hitting her name, I put the phone to my ear as it started ringing.

On the third ring, I heard Sky's voice on the other end answer.

"Sky?" I said in a low monotone.

I was nervous as hell.

"Who is this?" she asked.

"Uh, it's me, Isis." I replied.

"Oh my God, Isis! Are you okay? I'm so sorry!" Sky cried out into the phone.

She was throwing so many questions at me all at once that I didn't get a chance to get a word in. From the sound of things, she seemed like she was so worried about me.

"I'm okay Sky, how are you?" I asked her, trying to sound just as concerned about her.

I knew that I had to play this shit out if I wanted to find out all that I needed to know.

"I'm okay, where have you been?" she asked me in a shaky voice.

"I've been trying to lay low and figure out what the hell was going on. That day we got in an accident, I must have blacked out because I woke up in a hospital." I began to explain." "When I asked for you, the doctors kept telling me that I was the only one in the vehicle. I kept trying to call your phone, but I never got an answer. Then I started getting threatening calls from some dude, so I changed my phone number, which is the number I'm calling you from now." I told her.

The lies rolled off my tongue so damn smoothly that I was starting to believe this story my-damn-self. I sat on the phone for the next ten minutes or so, and listened to Sky cry and apologize to me repeatedly, saying everything was her fault. Funny thing was, she never once mentioned Gerald's name. Tired of hearing her voice, for now, I decided to get off the phone with her ass.

"Look Sky, I accept your apology. You've obviously been through a lot and so have I, but we're both safe now. How about I call you later and we can talk more?" I suggested.

"Yeah, that'll be cool, Isis. I'll talk to you later." Sky said and then we hung up.

I leaned my head back on the headrest and smiled. Seems like shit was going in my favor. Gerald's ass was dead and Sky didn't know that I was involved in him kidnapping her. The only thing I needed now to make all this shit sweet was time with Mr. Ronnie. Picking my phone back up, I sent him a text asking him if he wanted to come through the club tonight and chill for a while.

Hoping that he would respond telling me something I wanted to hear; I grabbed the rest of my things and headed back inside the club so that I could get this money, and soon enough, my man.

Chapter Twenty-Four

SKY

I just hung up the phone from speaking to Isis for the very first time since the accident. I was crying my eyes out, happy that my sister was okay. I was so afraid that she was lying somewhere dead, and it would have been because of me.

"You okay, Sky? What happened?" Katrice asked me as she came and sat next to me on the couch and wrapped her arm around me.

I laid my head on her shoulder and cried softly, while silently thanking God for sparing Isis' life. After a while, I sat back up, wiping the tears from my eyes and composing myself.

"I'm good now. That was my sister; she called to tell me that she was okay." I said to Katrice.

"Oh my God, that's good! Well, what did she say

happened? Like, how did she get out your truck? Where has she been?" Katrice asked me all at once.

We had already filled one another in on what had been going on with us individually these past couple of months. We both sat here and cried our eyes out for each other, sad for what we had to go through without us being there. I felt so bad. Not only for not being here for my best friend, but also hurting her with the things I was doing to myself.

"She said that she doesn't remember how she got out the truck, but that she must have blacked out because she woke up in the hospital. Then she said she kept asking for me, but the doctor told her that she was the only one in the vehicle. Shortly after, someone started calling her phone and making threats, so she changed her number." I explained to Katrice.

"Damn. That fool Gerald was really a crazy muthafucka!" Katrice shook her head.

"I knew that he had a thing for me because he never hid it; but I never gave Gerald any indication that I wanted to be with him. Then when he raped me, he took a piece of me that I knew I could never get back. I thought that by me being gone I wouldn't have to deal with his ass ever again in life! That nigga was obsessed with me since day one, and hated Ronnie just as much." This was the first time I openly spoke of the situation and even spoke Gerald's name out loud. I couldn't bring myself to speak on any of this, not even to the psychiatrist at the hospital. Ronnie and I never spoke about anything, and Ms. Mary said when I was ready to talk that she'd be waiting.

So, basically, I still had a lot of emotions and anger built up inside of me. Thank God I had Katrice now, though. We both apologized to one another for what happened and vowed to always be here from here on out; no matter what.

"Back to you, best friend." I changed the subject. "I'm so happy you are about to make me an auntie!" I smiled, rubbing her stomach.

When Katrice came over here, the first thing I noticed was her little baby bump. Since she was already what you called slim-thick, it was very noticeable. Soon as she came inside, we both hugged one another, crying. Not only did I not know that she was pregnant, but I also didn't know how serious she and Nick were.

"Girl, I'm trying my best to be happy, but muthafuckas just won't let me be great! I'm still sick as hell and now this shit is going on with Nick; I don't know whether I'm coming or going." Katrice expressed.

I like Nick, don't get me wrong, but I was feeling some type of way about the bullshit he had going on with Katrice and this other so-called baby momma he had out there.

"Well, do you think you're going to at least stick it out with him and see if this bitch's baby is really his or not? I mean, you did say that he said that he didn't know that she was pregnant. Besides, that hoe shakes her ass down at Coco's, so ain't no telling who the fuck she's been fucking." I said, trying to play devil's advocate in the situation.

Don't get it twisted, Nick's ass was still wrong for fucking with the hoe while he was with Katrice, but then again, I still think there's a strong possibility that this chick could be lying about being pregnant by him. Ain't no telling who her baby daddy could be.

"Hold up, Isis' ass danced at Coco's. What did you say this girl's name is again?" I asked Katrice.

"The bitch said Kim." she answered, rolling her eyes.

"When I talk to Isis again this week, I'll see if she knows her and get the tea on this hoe." I swear it was like Katrice and I fell right back into a routine with one another.

No matter what went down, me and her were riding for one other.

"Yeah, find out what you can for me. As far as me and Nick are concerned, I don't know, girl. Right now, I just don't trust his ass, so it's hard for me to try and go back to how things used to be with us. This shit looks messy as hell with two chicks walking around, pregnant from the same nigga. I can't be out here looking like no fool, Sky."

"But you're not. You're the one on his arm and the one that has his heart. Besides, you already know your newfound brother ain't gone let a nigga play you, regardless of who he is." I laughed.

It's funny how we can look at other people's situations and help them find a solution to their problem, but still can't solve our own shit. I was also still trying to digest the fact that Katrice and Ronnie were brother and sister. When Ronnie first told me that Katrice and Damon were his siblings, and how he found out about it, I looked at his ass like he was crazy. This shit felt like a big ass maze to me. My first love was one brother, then I ended up with the other brother, while best friends with the sister, only to go back to the first brother.

On the outside looking in, I would be labeled a hoe, but we already knew that was far from the case. Coming home, I felt like my life wasn't mine anymore. Everything that I thought I knew, I didn't. Nothing was the same. My daughter seemed like she was hesitant to be around me. I could reach for Imani and she'll either go to Ronnie or Ms. Mary instead.

They both tried to assure me that she just needed time to get used to me again, but what momma wanted to hear that shit? Then there was me and Ronnie; we weren't even sleeping in the same damn bed. We only spoke to one another if it was necessary and pretty much stayed out of each other's way.

The only thing that seemed the same around here was Ms. Mary. She was still the same sweet, caring soul. I'm so grateful she's here because she was the only thing holding this house together.

"Girl, I still can't believe Ronnie's crazy ass is my brother. I wish I would have found this out a long time ago, maybe I wouldn't—" Katrice stopped talking and looked away from me.

She didn't have to say anything else because I already knew where this was going, and I wasn't up for discussing Damon's ass either.

"Now that Sweet Pea is down for her nap let's get this gumbo started." We looked up to see Ms. Mary coming back down the stairs. "Y'all ain't handicapped, meet me in the kitchen to help." she said to Katrice and me.

We both jumped up from the couch and went into the kitchen as instructed. Ms. Mary had already started pulling out all the ingredients and placing them on the counter.

"Sky, take the skillet out, pour the olive oil in it, and put in on the stove on medium so that it can get warm. Katrice, come over here and help me chop up these onions and bell peppers." she instructed us both.

All three of us were moving around the kitchen, preparing this bomb ass gumbo.

"So when y'all two gone stop being stubborn with those men and get y'all shit in order?" Ms. Mary blurted out.

I looked up, shocked. I had never heard her curse before now.

"Don't look at me like that, I got a little bit of swag in me." Ms. Mary joked when she noticed us looking at her.

I couldn't help but burst out laughing.

"But, on a serious note, y'all two need to stop this and let those boys be there for you." she spoke again.

"Ms. Mary, that's all I was doing! But then I find out that Nick cheated on me and has this other girl possibly pregnant, what am I supposed to do?" Katrice asked on the verge of tears.

"First off, you need to stop all this crying and get yourself a plan. Now Nick messed up, but he's owning up to it. I also see his good outweighing his bad. So, the next step for you is to decide what's best for you and that life you are carrying."

Ms. Mary pointed at Katrice's stomach. "It ain't the end of the world, child; you know how many women go through worse? You better pull them big girl panties up and show Nick and whoever this other young lady is that you are strong."

"And you." She turned her attention to me. "I know that you have been through the ringer, but you were broke baby, not broken. Ronnie walking around here scared and walking on egg shells. The whole time you were away, that man didn't know what to do with himself. He had to deal with baby girl's situation with your mom while not being able to help you. He was just as lost as you, baby, and still is, but somehow, you two still seem so far apart from one another." By the time Ms. Mary was done talking, Katrice and I both had tears coming down our face.

Everything she had just said was true. I wanted nothing more than to open up and let Ronnie in again, but I just didn't know how. Something was holding me back. No matter what anyone said, I still felt like he would be better off without me.

Chapter Twenty-Five
RONNIE

I was sitting at the table with Nick and Rob, staring at the note that was in front of me. When Nick and I pulled up to the spot in the city that got hit, Rob had already had shit cleared out. When we walked inside, two niggas were laid out; shot with bullet holes to the chest. One of the bodies had a note pinned to it that read: *tell Ronnie the games are just about to begin, see you soon.*

After reading the note, Nick, Rob, and I decided to go back to one of our duck off spots in Carol City. I called Zay also and had him and the rest of the boys come and tail us as we drove there, making sure no one else was following us. Now, we were all sitting here, trying to figure out who was calling my ass out of retirement.

"The only two muthafuckas that could tell us how all this shit went down are dead." Rob began to talk. "No one else knew that they were gonna be there because I had that shit closed for today. Those two niggas were only there to do inventory and bring me the stash from the house. Someone must have followed them." Rob sat there trying to make sense of this.

"Either that or you got another snake bitch in your circle." Nick spoke up.

I just sat there quiet, still observing the note. At this point, I didn't give a fuck who followed who or any other shit like that. These bitches called me out, so I was about to answer their asses.

"Who you think this could be, Ronnie?" Nick asked me.

Looking up, I smirked. "Shit, ain't no telling."

The last thing I had was fear in me, so whoever did this ain't do shit but piss me off. I was already dealing with things at home with me and Sky, and although I wanted to try and get shit back on track with us, right now, that was going to have to go back on the back burner.

"I do know one thing though." I spoke "This means that I might have to come out of retirement for a while. Rob, you still do ya thing; this shit is still yours, but I can't sit back and have muthafuckas out here gunning for me and not take care of it personally. We already know Gerald and Damon's ass are somewhere in hell, probably sucking each other's dick, so it ain't them; But, whoever this is, they've been in the background watching."

I may have been low-key and quiet, but that still didn't mean niggas didn't have it out for me. Shit, Gerald's ass proved that. But I already knew how the game went. No matter how many niggas I helped feed or put on, there was still muthafuckas out there willing to do whatever it took to take my spot. I may have said I was out of the game, but deep down, I knew the game wasn't done with me.

The three of us sat there for the next hour as we all came up with a game plan. The team knew that Nick and I were out and that Rob was the go-to man now, and that's how we were going to keep it. No one else, besides us, was going to know that Nick and I were back on the scene, even if it was only temporary.

"You know y'all don't have to do this, I can handle it." Rob told us as we got up to leave. "Nick about to have a baby out here, and I know you still trying to get shit situated at home with Sky and your daughter." Rob pointed out.

"Come on Rob, you already know I'm a man about mine first before anything. Nigga wanna call me out; ain't no pussy in my blood." I assured him.

"I'm not saying that, bruh, all I'm saying is that I know y'all got families now; that's all."

"I appreciate you looking out for us, but I'm gone handle this and be done for good." I said, not knowing if that was true or not.

"Alright, listen, after I have this meeting and see if anybody else knows what's going on, I'll hit y'all boys up." Rob said to Nick and me as we all headed out to our cars and left.

"So, you really have no idea who this could be?" Nick said as he drove off.

"Naw man, ain't no telling. Now I gotta worry about this shit on top of what I'm already dealing with. I can't let Sky know about this though; shit is already stiff as hell at home now as it is." I said, letting out a long sigh as I thought about home.

Speaking of home, I knew things weren't going to pick right up where we left off when Sky came home from the hospital, but I didn't expect it to be like this either. She acting as if she didn't want to have anything to do with me. Sky never looked me in the face, barely talked to me, and when I would come around her, she would make an excuse as to why she had to leave out the room. I have never been through any shit like this with a female avoiding me, and right now, I was feeling some type of way about it.

"Aye, did you check with Sky to see if Katrice's ass was still at your crib?" Nick asked, breaking me from my thoughts.

"Naw." I answered curtly.

"What's up with y'all two?" Nick questioned.

"Shit man, I don't know. I'm starting to think she doesn't wanna be fucked up with me, though."

"Man, that's bullshit. Lil sis just been through a lot; give her some time. My ass the one that has a bigger chance of my woman leaving me than you do." Nick said, trying to make light of the conversation.

For the rest of the drive, we were both quiet; into our own thoughts. When we pulled into my driveway, I heard Nick sigh in relief when he saw Katrice's car still parked at my house. Getting out, we walked up to the door and went inside.

The smell of something delicious being cooked instantly greeted us as soon as we walked in.

"Damn, that shit smells good. I forgot Ms. Mary said that she was cooking some seafood gumbo." I said as I went into the kitchen with Nick following behind me.

Walking in was a sight to see. Ms. Mary, Sky, and Katrice were sitting at the table laughing and eating with Imani in her high chair next to them. I walked over to my baby and picked her up.

"Daddy missed his baby." I said as I munched on her cheek, which caused her to laugh.

"About time y'all got here. Katrice 'bout done ate up all the gumbo." Ms. Mary teased.

"I can't help it Ms. Mary! Not only is this so good, but it's the first time since I've been pregnant that I'm able to eat something and keep it down." Katrice replied.

I cut my eyes over at Sky, who quickly looked away from me when she saw me look at her. I shook my head as I placed Imani back in her high chair and went over to the stove to fix me a plate. Tired of the awkwardness and silence just because Nick and I came into the room, I fixed me some gumbo and went into the living room to eat; where I turned the television on Sports Center.

Nick must have felt the vibe too, because he joined me in the living room. We both sat there, now full, watching NFL Sunday football highlights, when Sky came and put Imani on my lap.

"Ms. Mary decided to turn in early, and since you don't

fully trust me with my child yet, it's time for her bath." She stood in front of me.

I grabbed my baby girl and stared up at Sky, not saying anything. I refused to get into this; especially in front of Nick.

"Aye man, I'm about to get out of y'all space. I'mma holla at you later." Nick said as he stood up. "Give Uncle Nick high five lil munchkin." he said to Imani as held his hand out low, and Imani tapped it with her little hand, smiling.

"See you later sis." Nick kissed Sky on the cheek and left out the room.

"Sky, I'm about to go too, but I have my to-go plate. Call me." I heard Katrice yell out.

I stood up, holding Imani, walking past Sky, and went upstairs to get my baby ready for bed. Thirty minutes later, after Imani had her bath and I put her down for bed, I went into the master bedroom where Sky was in bed, leaning against the headboard, reading on her Kindle. Normally, I would stick my head into the room and tell her goodnight, then go to the guest room where I'd been sleeping, but I was tired of living like we were fucking roommates. Matter of fact, I was sick of this whole situation period!

While Sky was reading, I walked over to the walk-in closet and started taking my clothes off.

"What are you doing?" I heard Sky ask me.

I turned around and noticed her staring at me, now shirtless.

"I'm about to take a shower." I answered her as I walked into our master bath and turned on the shower.

Stepping into the shower, I allowed the hot water to beat down on my body as I leaned forward on the wall. Letting out a deep sigh, I started thinking about my life and the things that were happening in it. I was grateful for my beautiful daughter, but I hated the fact that her mother acted like she despised me. I wasn't the enemy, yet Sky was treating a nigga like I was shit.

Washing off, I got out of the shower and handled the rest of my hygiene. With my towel wrapped around my waist, I walked back into the room and went to lay in the bed next to Sky.

"Ronnie, uh, don't you sleep in the guest room?" Sky had the nerve to say to me as she put her Kindle down.

"Yeah, I sleep in the guest room. Matter of fact, I can sleep in every room in this muthafucka if I wanted to, but right now, I'm sleeping in my room, in my bed, with my woman. Is that a problem?" I turned and looked at Sky, waiting to hear her next response.

With all the shit I already had going on, I'd rather be in her pussy, tearing that ass up right now, instead of her sitting here questioning why the fuck I was in our damn bed.

Sky just rolled her eyes at me, as she put her Kindle down on her nightstand and rolled over on her side. Frustrated, I reached over, turned her over on her back and got on top of her.

"Ronnie, what the fuck are you doing?" she said a little too loud with shakiness in her voice.

I could tell she was scared, but I was the last person she needed to be afraid of.

"Why you keep treating me like this, Sky? I know shit has been bad for you, but you're not in this alone. I love you, baby, but you killing me!" I seethed through my teeth.

I didn't plan on being emotional tonight, but I missed Sky and I didn't know how much longer I could take things with the way they were going between us. She just laid there, staring up at me with those beautiful eyes, but I saw no life in them.

"I'm sorry." she finally spoke in a whisper.

I leaned down and started kissing her. When she didn't reject me, I stuck my tongue deeper in her mouth as she let out a small moan. I felt her body starting to relax with me still on top of her as we continued to kiss. I used my legs to spread hers apart and started sucking on her neck.

"Hmm." Sky moaned out louder.

Now sucking on her breasts, I trailed kisses down her body, past her navel as I lifted her legs on my shoulder. Licking her inner thighs, I blew on the middle of her opening. I swear Sky had the prettiest pussy I had ever seen. Opening her legs wider, I buried my face between her legs as I started licking her sweet spot. Sky arched her back as she grabbed the top of my head.

With her grinding her pussy into my mouth, I clamped down on her thighs tighter, making sure her ass couldn't run anywhere as I sucked harder on her clit. I removed one hand from her thigh and started fingering her pussy at the same time I was sucking on it. That shit always drove her ass crazy. Feeling her legs as they started to shake, I knew she was about to cum all down my throat, so I sucked on that pussy harder.

"Ah!" Sky moaned out as she came hard.

I welcomed my baby's juices as I tasted her. Making sure I swallowed every last drop, I made my way back up on top of her and slid my dick inside. The fact that her pussy was still tight as fuck almost caused me to cum right then and there. It had been a long time since I felt the inside of Sky and this shit felt like a nigga was finally home.

Even though the doctor cleared her a while back for having sex again since her STD cleared up, she still wasn't trying to give me any ass. I understood, though, especially with the shit she went through. Sky wrapped her legs around my waist as I got into my rhythm and started stroking.

"I missed the fuck out of your ass." I whispered in her ear.

"Let me show you how much I've missed you." Sky said as she unwrapped her leg from around me.

I already knew what time it was. We switched positions as she got on top of me and positioned herself to ride the fuck out this dick. I taught her well, so I knew what to expect. Sky rode dick like a pro! Placing her hands on my chest and leaning up, she started grinding her hips as her pussy gripped my dick.

This shit felt so good that my toes were already curling! Sky bounced up and down as I slapped her ass cheeks.

"Fuck!" I yelled out as I felt her pussy muscles tighten up around the head of my dick.

I took control and pumped faster, not giving a damn that she was on top, and exploded all inside of her. Sky came right behind as she fell onto my chest, both us breathing heavy. We just laid there, with her wrapped in my arms. It may have been a quick fuck, but that shit was good and long overdue.

"I miss you Sky. I miss us. I'm so sorry shit happened to you, but I promise you I would die protecting you and Imani." I spoke, assuring her as I kissed her on the top of her head.

"That's the thing, Ronnie." Sky began to say as she rolled off me. "You always have to bail me out of shit and I'm sick of it." she said, looking at me.

"I don't bail you out of anything; it's called having your back. That's what a man is supposed to do." I replied, sitting up.

"Ronnie, since we met, it's always been you looking after me. I love you, baby, but it's time I look out for myself."

"What the fuck you saying, Sky? Because right now, you talking in circles." I asked, getting irritated.

"Ronnie, believe me when I say that I love you with all my heart and appreciate everything you have done. I especially love the way you stepped up and became a father to Imani. But I need to get myself together so that I can be a better mother to our daughter and person." she explained.

"Sky, I'm not stopping you from doing that."

"Ronnie, how do you think it makes me feel when I have to have a fucking chaperone around when it comes to me being around my daughter? For these past couple of years, it has always been me and her. Granny left, my momma wasn't there, you left, but I always had my baby. Now, I can under-stand why you all act that way because of what I tried to do to myself, but that still doesn't excuse the fact of how I feel. I've gone through more things in my short life than people two times my age have experienced. I'm tired, Ronnie. Right now, I should be in college, pursuing my career, but instead, I'm walking around here feeling sorry for myself. I need to be on my own and stand, baby...alone." Sky was now crying softly.

"So you saying you don't want to be with me anymore?" I questioned.

"I'm saying that I need some time and space to get myself together." she answered me.

I already knew what she meant; I just wanted to hear that shit come out her mouth.

"Aight, you want time, since it's obvious I'm stopping you from having that, then you got it." I jumped up and went into the bathroom to take a quick wash off.

As soon as I was done, I came out to find Sky still laying down in the bed, still crying. Ignoring her and her fake ass tears, I grabbed my briefs, basketball shorts, and t-shirt out of the drawer and put my clothes on. Once I was dressed, I turned around to address Sky one last time.

"I'm about to give you all the space you want, but you ain't keeping my daughter from me. You, Imani, and Ms. Mary can stay here; I'll leave and take care of everything just as I've been doing. No matter what, you and Imani will always be taken care of. I never want to hold you back, so if me leaving you alone helps make you a better person, then so be it."

Refusing to look her way, I left out of the room and went down the hall, back to the guest room; slamming the door. I was hurt and fucked up about what had just happened. I also felt like I had been played. All the shit I did for Sky, I did because I loved her ass and now she felt the need to want space from me to get herself together as she put it. Well, she was about to have all the muthafuckin space she wanted; I was done chasing her ass.

Chapter Twenty-Six

NICK

Man, I got myself in this situation that I don't even think Jesus Christ Himself could get me out of. How the fuck could I be so stupid to not only fuck with Kim's hoe ass, but to also think that she would get an abortion with the money I gave her? To make matters worse, Katrice still wasn't talking to me. We were on our way to her doctor's appointment to find out what we're having.

This was supposed to be a happy time; instead, her stubborn ass just stared out the passenger window, not paying my ass attention.

"You excited to see what we having, baby?" I asked her, trying to get her to talk to me.

"Yup." she answered, giving me these one-word answers. She's been doing that shit every time I try to make conversation with her.

Catching the hint that she didn't want to be bothered, I drove the rest of the way there in silence. When we pulled up to the doctor's office, Katrice got out of the car and began to walk inside by herself, leaving me to walk behind her. I ain't gone lie, the view of her ass from the back caused my dick to get on hard. Since she's been pregnant, Katrice put on weight in all the right places.

If she weren't so pissed at me, I would drag her ass back inside my car and fuck the shit out of her. Following close behind her, we walked inside and Katrice signed in. I took a seat, expecting her to sit next to me, but instead, Katrice sat across from me and picked up a magazine. I pulled my phone out and started checking my emails and social media messages to kill some time.

As usual, my inboxes on Facebook and DMs on Instagram were full of hoes leaving me their numbers, pussy screenshots, and other shit, trying to get me to fuck with them. While I was erasing my Facebook messages, I noticed that Kim had written me in my inbox.

Nick, I figured this was the only way I could say what I needed to say since you won't answer my phone calls or text messages. First off, let me start off by saying that I'm sorry for not going through with the abortion and popping up at your house. I was just hurt that you wanted me to get rid of my baby and not have anything to do with me anymore. I know that I'm not your woman, but I still thought that you would have at least had enough respect for me to let me make my own choice. I never had my momma there for me, and don't even know who the fuck my daddy is. I've been out here getting it on my own with no help or handouts from anybody. I'm having this baby for me, not you or anyone else. I don't want shit from you but to acknowledge this child because we both had a hand in creating HER! I won't bother you, but I do hope we can be adults and co-parent...holla at me when you ready to talk.

I stared at the message Kim had written me and was starting to feel a little bad at how I just left her hanging. I still had my doubts about whether the baby was mine and still planned on getting a DNA test when she had her, but until then, I do need to man up and make sure the baby was straight. *Her.* So, if this baby was mine, I would have a daughter.

"Katrice Williams" the nurse called out.

I looked up to see Katrice standing up and heading to the back. I put my phone back in my pocket and followed behind her. Once we got in the room, the nurse gave her a gown to change into, and informed us that the doctor would be in shortly. Closing the door and leaving us alone, Katrice started undressing and putting the gown on. I just stared at her and how beautiful her body looked.

There was no way in hell I was about to let another nigga touch all over that, so I had to do whatever it took to make sure Katrice's ass didn't leave me. Hearing a light knock on the door, the doctor came in smiling.

"Hello Katrice, today's the day!" the doctor said as she entered the room.

"I know, I'm so excited, Dr. Sandra." Katrice smiled as she laid back on the table.

This was the first time I saw my baby smile in a while. That shit made me feel some type of way that I wasn't the one who caused it, though.

"You must be Dad; I'm Dr. Sandra." The doctor held out her hand, introducing herself, with me returning the gesture.

"Okay, let's see if Mommy will be putting bows in the hair or if Dad will be playing catch." Dr. Sandra joked.

Katrice laid down on the table and Dr. Sandra opened the front of her gown and spread some jelly on her stomach. Grabbing that microphone looking shit off the machine, she placed it on Katrice's stomach.

Suddenly, there was a loud ass thumping sound, indicating that my baby's heart was beating.

"The heartbeat is good and strong, and from the looks of it, Dad will be playing catch and going to get haircuts!" Dr. Sandra said excited, indicating that we were having a boy.

It didn't matter to me whether we were having a boy or girl, long as the baby was healthy. But, now that I knew that I was about to have my first son, this made me even happier. I grabbed hold of Katrice's hand, shocked that she let me. Dr. Sandra gave us each copies of our sonogram pictures, and instructed Katrice to stop by the front desk to make her next appointment, and left out the room.

I continued to look at the first picture of my son, while Katrice got dressed.

"You ready?" Katrice asked, standing in front of me.

"Yeah baby, let's go." I stood up and allowed Katrice to walk ahead of me.

We stopped by the front desk on the way out so that she could make her next appointment, and left. When we reached my car, I hit the alarm and opened her door for her to get inside. I went around to the driver side and got in as well. Cranking the car up, I sat there for a minute before pulling off.

"We can't keep this up Katrice. If I have to, I will spend the rest of my life apologizing for what I've done. But I refuse to let my son come into this world in this fucked up situation." I turned to face her.

"This is a situation you created Nick, not me!" Katrice yelled out, looking at me.

"I know I did, and I'll do whatever is necessary to make this right. But you must still love my ass because you haven't left me, and I don't want you to leave. I just found out that you're about to give me my first son, a junior. I want my family home with me, Katrice." I begged.

I meant every word. Regardless of whoever else would be carrying my child, Katrice and my son were home. She stared at me, not saying anything as the tears started rolling down her face. Sitting here watching her cry from my wrongdoing was tearing me up inside. I went to reach over and try to touch her, but she yanked back from me.

"Do you know how that shit felt to find out that not only did you cheat on me, but that you could possibly have another baby out here with someone else? I felt like one of my lungs wasn't functioning. I couldn't breathe, Nick. My world came to a halt. You were the only one, besides my baby, that was the most stable thing in my life. I trusted you. Trusted you not to hurt me, but you blew it. I don't know what the future may hold for us, and I don't want our son coming into this situation either because it is unhealthy. You have to fix this, not me! I just need to focus on being stress-free so that I can bring a healthy child into this world. I will tell you this, though; if you still wanna be out here fucking these nasty hoes and making other babies, then you definitely won't have to worry about me." I saw the passion and seriousness in her eyes as she stared at me.

"I promise baby. I'll make it right, just give me a chance; but I do need to be around and see if the baby Kim is carrying is mine also."

"So you still trying to see that bitch!" Katrice yelled out again.

"Fuck no! I'm just trying to do the right thing and be there for the baby. I'm not the type of man that runs out on his responsibility, no matter what the circumstances are. I refuse to be that fuck nigga that has a jit out here and is not feeding it. This has nothing to do with Kim, only the child." I clarified.

Like I said, I loved Katrice and would do whatever I had to, to make sure things got back on track with us again, but an innocent child doesn't need to pay for my fuck up. Katrice looked at me, but I couldn't read her facial expression.

"Can we just go and get something to eat? I have a taste for some Red Lobster." She rolled her eyes at me.

I laughed at how stubborn her ass was. Before getting

Chapter Twenty-Seven

ISIS

I gave myself a look over in the full-length mirror and smiled. I was wearing tight-fitted skinny jeans that hugged my ass as if they were painted on, with a white short sleeved sheer shirt, my black lace bra showing, and a pair of black Michael Kors pumps. Earlier, I got a fresh wash and wrap from the Dominican beauty salon I go to; my nails, feet, and eyebrows were taken care of as well.

I had been planning for this day all week, and I wasn't about to be half-stepping. Grabbing my oversized Michael Kors hobo bag, I threw in an extra pair of panties, and grabbed an extra toothbrush out of my top dresser drawer. Snatching up my keys, I left out of my bedroom.

"Where the fuck you going? I'm not up for watching no damn kids tonight!" my momma yelled as soon as she saw me heading towards the front door to leave.

"I told yo' ass earlier that I had a date!" I said as I stopped walking and turned around to look at her ass.

I wasn't about to let her fuck my night up, especially since I was the one who planned on doing the fucking tonight.

"I don't give a fuck what you told me! Date my ass. Knowing you, you probably heading out to fuck somebody's husband or man. I ain't watching no damn kids either; I'm not feeling good and don't feel like being bothered." Evelyn stated as she tried to sit up on the couch.

I didn't give a fuck if this bitch had been run over by a truck, and only had one functioning arm working, I was not about to miss out on this opportunity to finally go out with Ronnie. That's right, my soon-to-be man had been hitting me up for the past two weeks, and we've been kicking it heavy on the phone. Now, I was about to go over to his place for the first time so that we could *chill*.

"Look Momma, I made these plans a week ago, and it doesn't matter who I'm fucking, as long as I paid you to watch my damn kids, you shouldn't have shit to say. If you don't feel like watching them tonight, then give me back my fucking two hundred dollars I gave you." I bluffed, holding my hand out.

Trust me, I already knew her ass wasn't about to give me my money back. Hell, I could bet anything she already spent it.

"Whatever. Just bring yo' ass back here tonight and get these damn kids because I ain't getting up in the morning, fixing no damn breakfast." Evelyn sucked her teeth and laid back down on the couch.

I walked out of the door and jumped in my car. Taking my phone out of my bag, I punched the address Ronnie texted me earlier into my GPS. Sending him a quick text, letting him know that I was on my way, I pulled off.

"You ain't gotta go home tonight, you can stay right here with me
I ain't going nowhere, when you wake up I'm gonna be right here
Don't you worry 'bout a thing, I ain't worried about shit
You're here with me, look it's like I love my wife, we going through things and I ain't going home tonight alright"

I was jamming to DMX and Monica's song, Don't Gotta Go Home, driving; the perfect anthem for me right now. When Ronnie hit me up a couple of weeks ago, I was shocked. Mainly because I'm the one that's always reaching out to him first. The initial conversation was light and short, but as time went on, they started to become longer, and then personal. That's when I learned that him and his daughter's mother, as he put it, weren't together anymore and that he was now living by himself.

That shit was music to my ears hearing that he and Sky weren't kicking it anymore. So, of course, I played the good friend and listened to him complain about how he was tired of chasing behind her and wanted to be with someone who appreciated him more. I told his ass everything he wanted to hear, gassing him up, and now I was on my way to his place to give him the best pussy he would ever have in his fucking life.

Lost in my thoughts, I didn't even notice that I was turning into the gated community. Pulling up to the guard gate, I gave the security my name and a copy of my driver license. After he called Ronnie to verify that he was expecting a visit from me, they let me in the gate. Still following my GPS, I drove to the end of the cul-de-sac and parked in front of a two-story house.

Cutting my car off, I grabbed my bag and got out. Walking up to the door, I rang the doorbell. While waiting on Ronnie to answer, I looked around and saw how perfect this neighborhood looked. All the yards had green grass and were cut. The houses were placed close together; this neighborhood looked like some shit that only white folks would live in.

Finally opening the door, Ronnie stood there in a wife beater and a pair of grey pants. I cut my eyes down low to see his dick print in full view. Quickly looking back up, I walked inside as Ronnie closed the door behind me.

"What's up lil momma?" he greeted me as he pulled me into a hug.

Lawd, this man smelled so fucking good that my pussy started jumping! I swear I almost melted in his arms.

"I'm good, how you doing?" I asked as I pulled away from him.

"I'm chilling; you look sexy as fuck." he complimented as he looked me up and down.

"Thanks boo." I replied as he grabbed my hand and led me into the kitchen with him.

When we walked in the kitchen, I noticed that he was cooking. Looking around, the kitchen had stainless steel appliances and Cherrywood cabinets. There was a pot of noodles boiling on the stove with ground beef in a pan simmering. *Good thing his ass knows how to cook because I won't be doing that shit,* I thought to myself.

"Do you want something to drink while I finish cooking the food?" Ronnie offered.

"Sure, what do you have?"

"I got some water, ginger ale, Gatorade, and Heineken." He said as he was looking in the refrigerator.

"Do you have anything stronger?" I asked.

"Oh, you trying to be a big girl tonight." Ronnie teased. "I got Cîroc, Hennessy, Coconut Rum, and some other shit at my bar in the living room. You're welcome to go help yourself while I finish cooking."

I walked out of the kitchen and into the living room, looking around. You could tell this was a bachelor pad. Ronnie had a black leather couch and loveseat, a big ass television mounted on the wall, and a glass coffee table sitting in the middle of the floor with a big picture of Imani sitting on top of it. Now that I think about it, looking at her picture, Imani does look a lot like Ronnie. Looking in the corner, I saw the glass bar, stocked with liquor and a huge ass fish tank sitting next to it.

I walked over to the bar and poured me some Hennessey, straight, then put some ice in my glass from the mini freezer next to the bar. After I had fixed my drink, I walked back into the kitchen to see what Ronnie was doing. He was taking bread out of the oven as I took a seat on top of the counter next to the stove.

"I see you drinking that grown man shit." He noticed me taking a sip from my glass.

"I'm fully grown, so that means I'm entitled to have this drink." I flirted.

"I can see just how grown you are." Ronnie flirted back. "Let's eat so you can put some food on that liquor."

Ronnie fixed our plates, and we sat down at the table to eat.

"Hmm, this tastes good." I said as I put a fork full of spaghetti in my mouth.

One thing about me, I was never the type of bitch who thought that she was too cute to eat in front of a nigga. Besides money and dick, food was my next favorite thing.

"I do a lil something in the kitchen. What about you, can you cook?" Ronnie asked as he took a bite of his own food.

"Hell yeah, I can throw down." I lied.

If you think I was about to tell this fine, sexy, paid, boss ass nigga sitting next to me that I couldn't cook, you had me fucked up. Besides, by the time he realized that I was all talk, my pussy would be more than a distraction to have him forget about it.

"So how's your mom doing, Ebony?" Ronnie asked.

I had him thinking that the only reason I stripped at the club was because my momma was handicapped and I had to take care of her.

"She's better. How is everything going with your daughter?" I switched the subject quickly.

"Good, I get her this weekend." he answered.

"So I take it everything with you and her mom is all good?" I probed.

"We co-parent. Nothing more, nothing less."

The rest of the conversation was basically him asking me questions about myself, and me lying my ass off, as usual. Once we were done eating, I offered to wash the dishes since he cooked. I'll be glad when I can stop with this good, wholesome girl bullshit. I haven't washed a dish in years. When I finished up in the kitchen, I went into the living room to find Ronnie's fine ass sitting on the couch, watching TV with his feet up on the table, and a glass of what looked to be Hennessey of his own in his hand.

"All done." I announced as I sat next to him on the couch.

"Thanks, even though you didn't have to clean the kitchen. I would have handled it." Ronnie sat up and placed his glass down on the table and reached for the blunt in the ashtray. Leaning back, he lit it up and took a pull from it.

"You smoke?" he asked as he held the blunt out in my direction, offering it to me.

"Only the good shit." I answered as I took it from his hand and put it to my mouth.

"Shit, I only fuck with the best." he laughed.

I inhaled and held it for a moment, then released the smoke and felt at ease. Already I could tell this was some good ass weed. For the next hour, we sat there getting high and tipsy, laughing our asses off at Kevin Hart on the TV. I had already taken my shoes off and had my feet propped up on Ronnie's lap.

The more I kept looking at him, the hornier I became.

"So, what is it that you're looking for Ronnie?" I asked him.

At this point, his ass could tell me that all he wanted was for me to suck his dick and I'd be down. I was feening for him and didn't know how much longer I could hold out.

"Right now, I ain't looking for nothing more than a friend. Someone that I can kick it with from time to time with no strings attached." he replied, looking over at me with his eyes sitting low.

"In other words, you looking for a fuck buddy?" I got straight to the point.

If the money was right, I wouldn't give a damn and would be happy to be this nigga's booty call, but I refused to settle with just fucking him for some chump change. I was gunning for the position to be the bitch that stood next to his ass.

"Like I said, someone I can kick it with from time to time. We grown, so if fucking come into play, then so be it." Ronnie said again, licking his lips.

Between the mixture of alcohol and weed, I couldn't hold back anymore. I leaned over to him and started licking on his neck. I lifted his shirt up, bent down, and started licking on his chest. I traveled down to his navel, licking it as well as I stuck my hand in his sweat pants. Pulling his dick out, I grinned and my mouth got watery as I held his thick, long dick in my hand.

I put the head of his dick in my mouth and started sucking on it. Just to give him a little tease, I continued to suck on the head while jacking his dick at the same time. Looking up at him, I smiled when I saw his eyes closed and head leaned back on the couch. *Now it's time to show his ass what I'm really working with.* I opened my mouth wider and took him whole.

"Shit." I heard Ronnie let out.

I started acting as if I was a fucking vacuum cleaner with the way I sucked on his dick. Not gagging once, as I felt him touch the back of my throat.

"Damn, Ebony!" Ronnie moaned out loud as he grabbed a hand full of my hair, as my head bounced up and down.

I propped up on my knees on the couch, and put my ass in the air while I continued to give him head. He started moving his hips and pumping faster, fucking my mouth. Ronnie tasted so good that I couldn't help but make moaning sounds. Feeling his thrusts going faster, I knew he was about to cum, so I sucked harder. Sure enough, he let out a grunt as he came all down my throat.

I continued to suck his ass dry, making sure I didn't waste a drop.

"Damn girl, hold up." Ronnie said in labored breaths, moving me slightly away from his dick.

I sat up, smiling and licking my lips.

"That ain't shit compared to what I can really do." I said

as I stood up, hoping he caught the hint that I was ready to fuck.

As if he was reading my mind, Ronnie stood up also, grabbed my hand, and led me up the stairs. When we got to his bedroom, he cut on his surround sound and R. Kelly played through the speakers. He took off all his clothes and laid on the bed, leaning up on his elbows. I swear to God those clothes did this man no justice!

I stood at the foot of the bed and did a little strip tease out of my clothes. When I was done, Ronnie reached into the nightstand drawer and pulled a condom out and put it on. I had the intention to not only have his ass fill my mouth up with his babies, but my pussy too. But that'll happen soon enough. Right now, I was about to take this nigga on a ride his ass had never been on before.

Chapter Twenty-Eight

KIM

I guess me leaving a message in Nick's inbox on Facebook must have worked because he called me earlier saying that he wanted to come over to talk. Of course, I agreed, in hopes that his ass would come over here and tell me what it is that I wanted to hear. Secretly, for the past two weeks, I had been doing a drive-by his house and following his bitch whenever she left the house.

I didn't know how far along she was, but I was now six months, and she was just as big as I was. Seeing how she looked caused me to be a little jealous, though. She was bad, in a natural state, which reminded me of Sky. There was no doubt that she was beautiful so I could understand why Nick's ass was with her, but in my eyes, she was still no competition to me.

I looked over at the clock and saw that Nick would be in

here in an hour. Since I already cleaned up earlier, I went and jumped in the shower. I tried my best to shave up since it was hard for me to bend down and see my pussy. After I was done showering, I got out and dried off. Back in my bedroom, I lotioned my body up with my Victoria's Secret body cream, putting cocoa butter lotion on my stomach. I decided to wear some boy shorts, showing my round stomach, and a cami top.

I put my versatile sew-in in a high ponytail; it looked like my natural hair. I sprayed a little of my Gucci perfume on so that it wouldn't be noticeable that I had just sprayed it. Right when I was finishing up, I heard a knock on my door. Smiling, I went out into the living room to answer the door. When I opened it up, there stood my possible baby daddy, looking yummy as ever.

"What's up?" Nick said as he walked past me and went to sit on the couch.

"Hey." I spoke back as I closed the door.

I switched my ass extra hard walking over to the couch from where he was sitting, giving him a full view. Sitting down across from him, I sat with my legs spread open, my pussy print on full display. Just like I thought, Nick's ass couldn't help but stare at it.

"So, what is it that you wanna talk about?" I asked.

"We need to talk about this baby situation." he answered, diverting his eyes back up to me.

"Okay, talk." I tried my best not to sound uninterested, but right now, this damn baby was the last thing I wanted to discuss.

"It was fucked up how you lied to a nigga and said you were getting an abortion when you didn't." he started off. "But it's too late to dwell on that, so here's how it's gonna be until you have the baby. Me and you won't be fucking around, that shit is dead, and so is that club shit for now. I'll take care of your lil bills that you have around here." He said, looking around my apartment. "As far as doctor's appointments go, keep me informed and I'll try my best to make them. How far along are you?" Nick asked.

"Six months." I informed him.

He didn't say anything for a couple of minutes, just stared down at my stomach.

"Like I said, I'll be taking care of your bills and things you need for her until she's born, and I will be getting a fucking DNA." He stated.

"Oh, so you must be getting a DNA test for your other bitch's baby too!" I blurted out.

I didn't mean to take it there, but this nigga was pissing me off. Already acting as if I wasn't shit and it was just going to be about this baby. I didn't give a fuck what he said; right now, this baby and me were a package deal!

"Whatever the fuck I got going on outside of you ain't yo' fucking business! And you need to watch your mouth when addressing my woman."

I couldn't believe Nick was sitting in my shit defending another bitch. Had this been any other nigga, I would have put his ass clean out. I had to quickly regain my self-control, and remind myself that for the next three months or so, he was going to be my meal ticket.

"I'm sorry Nick; it's these damn hormones. Nowadays, I'm just so emotional." I played it off.

"Here." He stood up and placed a wad of cash on the side table. "This is to take care of things you need to handle right now. Only call me if it's important and don't pop up at my crib again. I'm not about to have you and my lady going at it over no dumb shit." Nick walked towards the front door and opened to leave, but stopped and looked back at me.

"One more thing. I'm sure you heard about what type of nigga I am, but trust me when I say, you don't want to find out. You finding out where I stay at; don't let that shit get you get fucked up, pregnant or not. If the baby turns out not to be mine, consider the shit I did a fucking tax write off for yo' ass. I don't do drama, Kim." Nick gave me a hard look that caused me to look away from him.

He left out and closed the door. I continued to sit on the couch and digest everything he had just told me. I already knew messing with Nick in the wrong way could cause me to get fucked up, but if I played my cards right, I wouldn't have to worry about that. Finally getting up, I went over to the table where he dropped the money and picked it up.

After counting it up, I learned that it was a total of five thousand dollars. *Damn, I can get used to this*. Smiling, I took the money and went to put it in my stash spot back in my bedroom. Nick may have satisfied one of my cravings, and that was by leaving me some cash, but I still wished he would have broken me off some of that good ass dick he had.

Putting my money away, I grabbed my cell phone and looked through my contacts to dial up one of my other potential baby daddy's. Shit, ain't no telling who my real baby daddy was, but somebody was about to feed my seed now.

Chapter Twenty-Nine
SKY

It had been almost a month since Ronnie moved out, and I was still trying to get used to the way things were between us now. He made good on his word and had been taking care of us and the household financial wise, but I wouldn't have expected anything less of him. He also called for Imani every evening and had plans on getting her this weekend so that he could spend some time with her at his new place.

Other than discussing the well-being of our daughter, we don't talk. When I said I wanted space to get myself together, I didn't expect him to totally pull away from me. I rolled over in my bed and saw that Imani was still asleep. She'd been sleeping with me since Ronnie left, and I enjoyed every minute of it; reminded me of old times.

Kissing her lightly on her face, I got out of bed and went

into the bathroom to handle my morning hygiene. After peeing, I stood at the sink and looked at myself in the mirror. I was starting to look like my old self again. My acne cleared up and my skin wasn't ashy looking anymore. I had even been going back to the salon to get my hair treated.

I was also putting weight back on, which wasn't hard since Ms. Mary cooked Sunday dinners damn near every night. Once I was done brushing my teeth and washing my face, I went back into the room to see Imani sitting up in the middle of the bed. Soon as she saw me, she reached out her little hands.

"Good morning, mommy's baby." I cooed as I went over to the bed and scooped her up.

The only good thing that came from Ronnie leaving was the fact that I didn't feel like I had to be watched around my daughter. Imani seemed to have grown closer to me, and I loved it. I took her into the bathroom as well to wash her little face, brush her teeth, and change her out of her pull-up, which was dry, so I sat her on the toilet for a while.

We were in the potty-training stages, and so far, my baby had been rocking this shit. After wiping her clean when she was done and putting her on a new pull-up, we headed downstairs to get our day started. Just as expected, Ms. Mary was in the kitchen, cooking breakfast.

"Good morning babies, how'd you sleep?" she greeted us as I went to the kitchen and put Imani in her high chair.

"We slept well, how about you?" I asked, opening the refrigerator and taking out the apple juice.

Grabbing one of Imani's sippy cups down from the cabinet, I poured the juice in there and handed it to her.

"I slept good, but it would have been better if I had a man lying next to me." Ms. Mary said as she bent down to take the biscuits out of the oven.

I burst out laughing at what I had just heard. I couldn't believe some of the things that came out of her mouth most of the times.

"Don't act like you don't feel the same way." she said, looking at me.

I knew where she was going with this. Ever since Ronnie had been gone, Ms. Mary hadn't directly spoken on it, but she had been making little comments here and there. I knew it would be a matter of time before she wouldn't be able to hold her tongue much longer, though.

"Well, I don't need a man to sleep next to me when I have my princess over there." I cut my eyes over at Imani, who was drinking from her cup and not paying us any mind.

"Now you know I try to let y'all young folks handle your business, but I can't keep being quiet about this. You said that you needed space from Ronnie to get yourself together, but what have you done since he's been gone?"

"What do you mean?" I asked, confused as to what she had just said.

"What are you doing now that is so different that you couldn't do when he was here?" Ms. Mary clarified, asking me again.

"Ms. Mary, I was tired of depending on Ronnie and always

having him coming to my rescue. I need to stand on my own so that I can be able to take care of me and Imani." I tried my best to explain.

"And that's fine, baby." Ms. Mary walked over to the table and took a seat next to me. "But you don't have to be alone to be able to stand on your own. That man loves you and his daughter with everything in him and has shown it time and time again, and he's been patient. I may not have a man now, but believe me when I say, I have had more than my share back in the days. If you continue to push a man away, he gone go right into the arms of another heffa waiting on him." Ms. Mary stood back up and went back over to the stove to fix our plates.

I sat there for the next ten minutes, picking at my plate while feeding Imani grits. There was no way I wanted Ronnie to be with another chick, but the way he had been acting lately, I didn't know if it was too late to be worried about that now.

"I've been thinking" I spoke. "I think I'm going to sign up for classes at Nova Southeastern University. It's not that far from home, and school was my initial plan."

"That's good!" Ms. Mary said, enthused as she patted me on my back.

"Yeah, you're the first person I told. I had plans on tell Ronnie but..." I cut myself off.

"Anyway, Katrice and I are going to the mall today. She wants to get some stuff for the baby, and I'll be picking Imani

up some things as well. You wanna come with us, Ms. Mary?"
I offered.

It was Friday, and I didn't want her sitting in the house
while we were gone. Bad enough she was still on a leave of
absence from the hospital babysitting me.

"No, y'all gone on ahead. I have to meet with human
resources at the hospital today."

"Are you going back to work?" I asked.

"No. Actually, I'm turning in my packet to retire. I've been
doing nursing now for about twenty years and I'm still considered young, so I think it's time that I retire and relax; enjoy
the fruits of my labor." Ms. Mary explained.

"Oh wow, I didn't know that you had plans to retire. I
hope that doesn't mean that you're leaving us." I replied in a
panic.

Ms. Mary had become my granny here on earth. I had
gotten so used to her being here for us and making sure that
we had stability in our house, just like Ronnie. *Damn, there
wasn't a difference from when he was here.*

"Eventually, I will, but not now." Ms. Mary assured me.

Once we all finished breakfast, I got Imani and I dressed.
Katrice was meeting us here at my house and then we were all
going to the mall together. An hour later, Katrice was ringing
the doorbell. When Imani and I got downstairs, Katrice's
greedy ass was standing at the kitchen counter, stuffing her
face.

"Damn girl, I swear your ass is always eating." I teased
when I got close to her.

Sure enough, her ass was eating on some of the leftover chili we had last night.

"So what! You already know Ms. Mary be throwing down and I got hungry on the way over here." she said with her mouth full.

I put Imani down and went to grab her snacks and juice box out of the refrigerator. By the time I got her bag ready, Katrice was done eating and we headed out the door. We jumped in my recent car, a Mercedes CLK that Ronnie got me, with Imani safely in her car seat. This was the first time I was driving since the accident, so I took a deep breath and turned to face Katrice.

"Which mall do you want to go to?" I asked her.

"How about we go to Pembroke Lakes Mall; They have a Babies "R" Us on the way there." Katrice suggested.

My hands got sweaty as I gripped the steering wheel. The last time I was heading to that area, I got kidnapped. Noticing how uncomfortable I had become, Katrice put her hand on my shoulder.

"My bad Sky; we don't have to go in that area."

"Nah, we good. I can't keep letting the past hinder me." I put my car in reverse and pulled out of my driveway, heading in the direction of the mall.

"Speaking of which, have you and Ronnie ever talked about what happened with buddy and the whole situation?" Katrice asked me, referring to Gerald.

"Not in details. The only thing he ever said to me about it was that I didn't have to worry about Gerald anymore. I didn't ask him to elaborate on it, and he didn't volunteer to."

"Well, I guess we both already know what that shit means." Katrice said in a low voice, but loud enough for me to hear.

"What's going on with you and Nick right now, though?" I changed the subject.

I refused to waste any more of my precious breath talking about the fuck nigga Gerald.

"Girl, he on some kumbaya type shit with me and this other hoe who might be pregnant by him." She sucked her teeth.

I know that Ronnie and I weren't in the best place right now, but I couldn't imagine how I would be dealing with the shit Katrice is dealing with right now.

"What you mean on some kumbaya type shit?" I laughed at the analogy she used.

"He's coming at me talking about how he didn't want any drama and that for the time being, he was gonna be there for the bitch's baby until he got a DNA test. When I asked him how far along she was, he had the nerve to tell me that she was six months!" Katrice yelled out.

I cut my eyes in the rearview mirror to make sure Imani was occupied and smiled when I saw her on her iPad.

"Wait, but you're almost six months too!" I pointed out.

"Exactly! I could have punched him right in his shit when he told me that! So, I'm back to walking around the house, ignoring his ass. I just don't know how I'm going to take sharing him with another bitch right now." Katrice shook her head as she looked out the passenger window.

I knew my best friend, and I could tell she was getting emotional, which is why she was avoiding eye contact right now. She hated to cry in front of people. Katrice was hurting and her pregnant hormones didn't make it any better.

"It's gonna be all good, best friend." I tried consoling her.

"But what if it isn't? What if her baby does turn out to be his? Nick is not a fucking deadbeat, so I know that he'll be there for her child, meaning her ass will be in the picture too. He cheated on me, and the longer I stick around, the more I have to look at his indiscretion in my face." She admitted, now crying.

"Well, if it comes to that, then that's when you have to decide if you want to raise a baby in an environment that you would be unhappy in. You don't have to be together to raise a healthy, happy child, Katrice, remember that."

The rest of the ride over to the mall, we talked about me signing up for college courses after the winter break, and Katrice joining me at the school as well after she had my nephew. Once we got to the mall, we valet parked and went inside. The first store we stopped in was Footlocker. I wanted to get me and Imani matching Adidas and buy Katrice's baby his first pair of Jordan's.

About an hour later, with Imani's rented stroller filled with bags, we decided to stop by the food court to get something to eat.

"I have a taste for some pizza." Katrice announced as she

headed in the direction of the pizza line, with me following behind her.

Once we got our food, we found a table and sat down to eat. I cut up a slice of pizza for Imani and began to feed her as I ate my own.

"Aye, you ever asked your sister about the Kim girl that worked down at the strip club with her?" Katrice asked me with her damn mouth full.

"No. Every time I try calling her, she doesn't answer. Then when I text her, she barely responds. I guess she went back to being the old Isis." I shrugged my shoulder as I took a sip of my Sprite.

As we were sitting there eating and talking, I looked around and someone caught my eye. I sat there, staring at the bitch, trying to contain myself from getting up and going over there to whoop her muthafuckin ass!

"I swear I've been waiting to see that bitch for the longest." I spoke.

"Who?" Katrice asked as she saw me looking over at the girl standing in the line at the food court.

"Remember when I told you how one of my homegirls from back in the day watched Gerald rape me?"

"Yeah." Katrice answered.

"Well, there goes that bitch right there in the red shirt." I pointed in Kim direction, who turned around just in time and looked dead in our direction.

"You gotta be fucking kidding me! That's the same hoe that came to our place and told me that Nick got her pregnant!" Katrice said out loud as we were both still looking at Kim.

She was with some other bitch and they both looked at us and smirked. I took notice of her stomach and couldn't believe this shit.

"Wait, that's the Kim?" I asked.

"Yeah, that's her!"

Kim and the chick walked past our table with their food like they didn't have a care in the world. I couldn't believe that's the Kim Nick fucked around with and got pregnant. The same slimy hoe that watched me get raped and tried to talk to Ronnie behind my back! Oh, Katrice had more than just a baby momma to worry about now.

Chapter Thirty

RONNIE

"So, you telling me that the person that came to the trap house and shot those fools up was a female?"

"Yeah, man. One of the lil niggas that was at there earlier that day said he had stopped by to do a drop-off. When he was leaving out, he saw this fine ass bitch walk past him and go inside. Anyway, when I asked him if he could remember what her face looked like, his dumb ass said no, he only paid attention to her ass, so you already know I handled his ass for slipping up like that and not paying attention to his fucking surroundings" Rob let me know.

"As you should have. Can't have niggas around that's not on their toes. Getting distracted by some ass will cause the whole ship to go down." I pointed out.

The more I hear Rob talk about how he's handling shit,

only confirms that Nick and I made the right choice in choosing him to take over.

"Shit, you already know how I'm rocking." Rob gave me a fist pump. "Anyway, I remembered nosey ass Candice who lived up the street with the video cameras outside her house. So, I went over there and shot her five hundred to give me the tape from that day. After she had given it to me, I took it back to my crib and started analyzing it. Here; I ended up getting some images from the video and blew them up." Rob slid some pictures across the table to me.

I stared at the pictures, looking at this chick. She was a bold bitch considering the fact she wasn't trying to hide her face; however, she looked so familiar to me.

"You recognize her?" I heard Rob ask me.

"She looks like I've seen her somewhere before, but I can't put my finger on it."

"Well, the fact that we know that it was a female gunning for us, makes it a little more complicated. I don't recall ever having to deal with a situation like this that involved a bitch, but she can't be working by herself." Rob speculated.

"Nothing is complicated, just a little challenge. But we don't discriminate because this hoe is about to get dealt with just like a nigga would. Did you get any other images, like a license plate number or the description of the car she was in?" I questioned, still studying the picture.

"I'm working on that now. In the meantime, shit still closed over there and I got extra niggas working and watching out for the other spots."

"Good. Whoever this hoe is, she needs to be dealt with ASAP." I leaned back in the chair and took a deep breath.

"You good?" Rob asked, noticing me looking off into space.

"I'm straight man. I just thought that with me getting out of the game, I would be more relaxed right now, but seems like it's the total opposite." I confessed.

"Aye man, like the old heads always say, once you in this shit, you in it for life. I'mma keep looking into this and get back to you as soon as I get some more info." Rob stood up and gave me a pound and he left out of the room.

We met up at the warehouse in Carol City early this morning. I was in my bed, sleep, with my dick still hanging out from the night before, when Rob called me, telling me that he had some info on who tried to knock off one of the spots. For the past month now, I had been fucking the shit out of Ebony. Almost every night when she got off work from the club, she would come by my place and we would fuck, drink, and smoke. Then, without being told, she would leave in the morning.

Right now, the little setup we had worked out for us, but truthfully, I was only using Ebony as a distraction from missing Sky's ass. I've been trying my best to avoid her if it doesn't concern Imani. I was beyond pissed at the way she just tossed my ass to the side as if I wasn't shit to her. If I were a woman, people would say that I was hurt, but I wasn't about to be walking around here crying and shit and begging someone who didn't want to be with me.

Instead, I only spoke to her ass when she called me about Imani or if I called her to speak to my daughter. Avoiding Sky right now was the only thing keeping me from lashing out at her. Right now, I was about to head out to the house to pick up Imani so that she could spend the weekend with me.

I left out of the warehouse and jumped in my truck. Soon as I was about to pull off, my phone vibrated. Looking at it, I saw that Ebony sent me a text message.

EBONY *I know I just left, but I'm still thinking about that good ass dick.*

Smiling, I sent her a text back.

ME *That's why you miss it because my shit legit lol.*

EBONY *W.E(whatever) I know you getting your daughter this weekend so holla at me when you can.*

ME *NP(no problem)*

Laying my phone on top of the middle console, I pulled off, heading to pick up Imani. After about twenty minutes, I pulled into my circular driveway, parking behind what looked to be Katrice's car. Getting out, I went up to the front door and used my key to let myself inside.

I may not be living here now, but I'll be damn if I'm knocking on some shit I pay the bills on. Stepping inside, I could hear talking. Walking in further, I saw Sky and Katrice in the living room in a heated conversation. Sky was standing up in the middle of the floor while Katrice was sitting on the loveseat with her head down in her hands.

"I can't believe this shit! I bet you—" Sky stopped in the middle of going off when she saw me standing there.

Katrice noticed that Sky stopped talking as well and looked up. Rolling her eyes at me, she stood up and snatched up her purse.

"I'm about to head out Sky. I gotta handle this shit. I'll call you later." She walked past me without speaking and left out the house, slamming the fucking door.

"Where's Imani?" I asked Sky, who was still standing there with her arms folded across her chest, staring at me with a pissed off look on her face.

"She's upstairs napping, but before you take her, I need to ask you a serious fucking question, and I'd appreciate it if yo' ass doesn't lie to me."

"When the fuck have I ever lied to you, Sky?"

She stood there looking at me for a few seconds before speaking.

"Did you know that the bitch Nick cheated on Katrice with and got pregnant was Kim that I used to roll with?" she asked me.

Fuck! I knew this shit was gone come out! I told that nigga to leave that hoe alone, and now that the full cat is out of the bag, Sky is standing here questioning me as if I'm the one that got Kim pregnant.

"Look Sky, you already know that I don't get in other people's shit, especially a grown ass man." I replied instead of answering the question.

"So, that means you did know then."

"All I know is that by the time Nick told me about this

situation with the bitch, it was too late. That man is grown Sky and that's for him and Katrice to deal with."

I wasn't about to keep standing here, getting interrogated about what another nigga did with his dick. I went into the kitchen to grab a water out of the refrigerator. I heard Sky following behind, which I expected. She had to get the last word in by any means, so this conversation wasn't over.

"I know Nick is a grown ass man, but Katrice is my fucking best friend! You of all people know how slimy that bitch Kim is, and now she's trying to pull this shit about being pregnant from Nick." Sky pointed out.

I leaned against the counter, opened my water, and took a swallow.

"How the fuck you know about Kim anyway?" I questioned.

"Because Katrice and I were at the mall earlier with Imani, shopping, when we saw the bitch at the food court. That's when Katrice pointed out that she was the one that came to their house and claimed that she was pregnant by Nick. Then the hoe had the nerve to walk past us smiling. Imani saved her fucking life today because had my baby not been there, I would be in jail right now for fucking that hoe up!" Sky was pissed, but she didn't need to be taking that shit out on me.

"Right now, I'm just trying to figure out why the hell you didn't tell me, Ronnie?"

"You act like we were walking around here holding conversations with one another. I was trying to make sure my own woman was straight before talking about another nigga and his household. And just like Katrice is yo' best friend, she's my sister and Nick is my boy." I reminded her.

By the look on Sky's face, I could tell her ass was stuck on what to say next. She left out of the kitchen, leaving me there, and headed up the stairs. Still standing in the kitchen, I honestly didn't want Nick and Katrice's problem to coincide with what Sky and I already had going on. Nick may be my boy, but this was one time he fucked up royally.

Lost in my thoughts, I looked up to see Sky coming back in the kitchen with a sleeping Imani on her shoulders with her little Tinker Bell duffle bag in tow as well.

"Here, I put extra clothes in there just in case you guys go somewhere. She is potty training, so I have pull-ups in there as well." Sky explained as she handed me Imani and her bag.

"Sky, stop talking to me as if I don't know my own fucking daughter." I suddenly became irritated at how she was coming at me.

"Whatever, just let me know if you're going to drop her back off or if you want me to pick her up." She said with attitude as she turned to walk out of the kitchen, but I lightly grabbed her on her arm, stopping her.

"Listen, I don't know what your problem is, but I'm not the enemy. You wanted this space shit, so I'm honoring it, but don't start treating me like a fuck nigga out here in these streets." We both stared at one another.

She looked down at my hand still holding on to her arm, and then back up at me. That was my cue to let her shit go, which I did.

"I'm not treating you like anything but the father to my child." Sky coldly said.

From the fuck shit that had just come out of her mouth, to the look in her eyes, it gave me all the confirmation that I needed on where we now stood.

"Aight, say no more. I'll bring Imani back Sunday afternoon." With that being said, I adjusted my baby in my arms and headed out the front door.

After securing Imani in her car seat, I got inside and pulled out the driveway. Before pulling off into the street, I called Ebony up right quick and asked her if she felt like chilling with me tonight. She agreed and told me that she'd see me later. Satisfied, I proceeded to drive off and head home. I love Sky, and always will, but I was done sitting around waiting for her ass to grow the fuck up.

Chapter Thirty-One

KATRICE

I sat outside in front of the house that Nick and I shared, parked behind his truck, trying to calm down before I went inside. After today, this would be the last time that I would step foot in this shit. I couldn't believe out of all bitches, he ended up fucking with Sky's ex-best friend. As of yet, I hadn't confirmed with him if he knew beforehand who she was or not, but I'm almost certain he did, especially since Ronnie knew about the bitch.

It took everything in me not to get up from the table we were sitting at in the food court earlier that day and mop the floor with that hoe's face when she passed by us smiling. So, since I couldn't get in her ass, Nick was about to be the next best thing. Besides, he was the cause of all this bullshit anyway! I called him on the way from Sky's house and asked him to meet me home ASAP.

Knowing him, he probably thought that something was wrong with the baby because I saw that he was already here. Grabbing my purse and bags from the mall, I got out the car and headed inside the house. As soon as I opened the door, Nick was coming towards the door.

"Let me get these bags from you baby." He offered as he took the shopping bags from me.

Closing the door, I rushed to the bathroom to pee because my baby was pressing on my bladder. Once I was done using the bathroom, I washed my hands and left out. As I was heading back out front, I overheard Nick on the phone.

"Man, what the fuck! Aw shit, aight." I heard him say.

Turning the corner, I saw Nick standing in the kitchen on his phone. He must have felt my presence, because as soon as I walked in, he turned around and looked at me.

"Aye, Ronnie, let me hit you back." He said quickly and then hung up the phone.

"So since that was Ronnie on the phone, I guess you already know why I asked you to come home." I spoke as I leaned against the island, facing him with my arms folded over my stomach.

Little did Nick know, regardless of what the fuck was about to come out of his mouth, it wouldn't make a difference because we were a wrap.

"I just found out what happened; I'm sorry Katrice." he sighed loudly, shaking his head.

"Nick, lately, that's all you have been—sorry. So, I guess

telling me the half-truth about this bitch was your way of trying to keep fucking with her ass?"

"Hell no! I meant what I said about only dealing with her ass concerning the baby until she's born." He protested.

"Oh she? Well, congrats on your daughter. I hope like hell she doesn't run into a lying, cheating, ass nigga like her daddy! The fact that you failed to tell me that this girl was the same bitch that crossed Sky is what confuses me; is it because you didn't know?" I asked, staring at him.

I honestly wanted to hear the truth out of his mouth. Putting his head down slightly and not answering me right away, already confirmed what I had thought earlier; his ass knew.

"Alright, look, Katrice. I'm trying my best to make this shit right so I'm not gone even lie to you. Yes, I knew who she was. Ronnie had already told me who she was the first time I saw her at the club." he admitted.

"But you fucked with her anyway, right? Fuck me and what we had going on. I swear I thought yo' ass was different, but like the saying goes, fool me once shame on you, fool me twice...you know the rest. Nick, I can't do this shit. Before you, I had a drama-free life with no worries. Now I'm pregnant and in love with a man who doesn't respect the value of a good woman. I will, in no shape or form, keep you away from your child, but this here," I pointed back and forth between us. "We are done." I finally told him, trying my best not to cry.

I loved Nick, but I refused to keep putting up with this.

One thing about me, I was all for loyalty, and once you fucked that up, you lost me. Nick stood there, staring at me, not saying anything.

"I'm gonna move in with Sky until I have the baby. Afterward, I'll get a place for us to stay. Like I said, I won't deprive you of anything concerning your son." I spoke again.

Nick walked over to the island where I was leaning and pulled me in his arms. I laid my head on his chest and started crying. This man had my heart, and I was about to have my first child from him, yet I felt like a part of me had just died.

"Katrice, I love you and only you. There is no way in hell that I'm about to let you walk out of my life and have my son grow up separately from me. If I have to, I'll give you a lifetime of apologies for this shit I created. I honestly can't make an excuse as to why I did what I did and with whom, but I can promise you that I will never do anything to intentionally hurt you again." Nick lifted my face up by my chin and looked me in my eyes.

"Please don't leave me, baby. Let me make my family whole again." Nick begged me.

The look in his eyes showed nothing but pure desperation. My mind was now in a race with my heart, and these damn hormones weren't helping any.

"Nick, I refuse to go through this. I already know this girl is gonna try and cause trouble. Look at how she fucked over Sky and tried to sleep with Ronnie. I mean she stood there and watched Gerald rape Sky the first time!"

"Wait, what?" Nick looked at me confused.

"Oh, you didn't know? The bitch is a snake and I'm not about to sit back and deal with her ass. If that baby turns out to be yours, then that means I will have to deal with her. I can't do it." I shook my head, backing away from his embrace.

"Okay, I can't do shit but respect how you feel, bae, but please don't leave home. I'll make sure no drama comes your way. I don't want to miss out on anything with my son." Nick rubbed my stomach, causing me to shiver.

He already knew the smallest touch caused me to go crazy and caused me to want to fuck the shit out of him. That's one of the perks of this pregnancy; I'm never too tired to fuck. I can go two to three times a day if I could.

"I swear I'll give you your space and won't keep you in the dark about shit else, but just stay." He asked me again.

Still not responding to him, Nick lifted me up on the counter and started kissing me on my neck. I closed my eyes and leaned my head back, letting out a soft moan. He knew that this was my spot, so right now, I didn't stand a chance. Opening my legs wider to invite him in, I wrapped them around his waist. I already had on a dress, so Nick already had easy access.

As if he read my mind, he quickly pulled down his shorts and slid inside me.

"Hmm," I moaned out.

Scooting my ass to the edge of the counter, I started thrusting my hips forward, throwing my pussy back. Nick pulled my breasts out and started sucking on them, which drove me crazy! My nipples were extra sensitive and the sensation of his lips wrapped around them was an unbeliev-able feeling.

"Damn, this pussy just got wetter." Nick observed as he sat up and grabbed hold of my ass cheeks.

"This pussy is so fucking good; you ain't going nowhere!" he said out loud, fucking me faster.

Wrapping my arms around his neck, I was holding on for dear life as he was now holding me in the air. This dick was so good that I felt my pussy juices gushing out of me.

"Damn baby, I love you!" I screamed out as I felt myself about to cum.

"You gone leave?" Nick asked, pumping faster.

"No, baby, I ain't going nowhere!" I yelled out.

"Oh God!" I screamed as I exploded.

"Um-huh, open yo' legs wider; I'm about to feed my seed." Nick ordered as he thrust harder.

"Ahh!" he finally yelled out as he came inside of me.

Still holding onto him, he placed me back on top of the counter, breathing heavy. I may have just cum, but my pussy was still throbbing.

"You still leaving?" Nick looked at me, trying to catch his breath.

"That depends on how good you tear this pussy up from the back," I replied, smirking as I got down off the counter and turned around.

What can I say, the pussy won over the heart and mind today.

Chapter Thirty-Two
ISIS

Things couldn't have been going any better than they were now between Ronnie and me. Yeah, we still weren't an official couple and he never took me out in public, but right now, I was willing to take whatever I could. We were chilling at his place, watching a movie on the couch. I was shocked as hell when he asked me to come over tonight, considering that he told me earlier that he was going to have Imani's ass this weekend.

Thank God she was asleep when I got here. The last thing I needed was for my niece to recognize who I was. Although she was still a baby, I still had to be careful. Since Imani was upstairs asleep, Ronnie wasn't allowing us to get fucked up like we normally do, so right now, we were both in a clear state of mind, meaning I had to be on my toes.

"So, do you have your daughter the whole weekend?" I asked, trying to start a conversation.

Since I came over, Ronnie had been quieter than usual. The movie *Love & Basketball* was on the television, but neither of us was paying that shit any attention.

"Yeah." he answered me short, still looking at the TV.

"What's wrong, Ronnie? Since I got here, you've been distant." I questioned as I turned my body to face him on the couch.

"I'm sorry about that. I just got a lot of shit on my mind right now." he confessed, looking at me.

Having him look at me right now caused my pussy to jump.

"Well, is it something you want to talk about?" I asked in hopes that he would say yes.

I didn't know if whatever he had going on involved Sky or not. She had been hitting me up lately, leaving me texts and voicemails, but I just ignored the shit. Honestly, I didn't want to deal with her, especially since I was fucking her baby daddy now. But if shit kept up like this, I might just have to backtrack and talk to the bitch just to keep tabs on what she and Ronnie had going on.

"Nah, I'll handle it." he replied instead.

I swear this dude had a real tight lid on his business.

"Well, how about I do something else to take your mind off whatever it is you're dealing with?" I offered, licking my lips.

"Oh, yeah?" Ronnie smiled. "You gotta be quiet 'cause you already know my daughter upstairs sleeping."

He sat up a little and pulled his sweat pants down. I straddled him with a skirt on and pulled my panties to the side, hoping that he wouldn't stop me this time with that getting a condom bullshit. We already fucked twice now without one, due to Ronnie's ass being too drunk to even take notice. When I went to slide down on his dick and noticed he didn't stop me, I took that as my cue to continue.

"Oh" I said in a low moan.

I had to bite my bottom lip to stop me from making loud sounds. Ronnie wrapped his arms around me, pulling me forward to lay on him, and started fucking me while I was on top of him. Grabbing onto the back of the couch, I positioned myself and started bouncing my ass up and down on his thick meat.

"Fuck girl, ride this dick!" Ronnie whispered.

I knew my riding skills were on point, so I did exactly what he asked of me. After about ten minutes of us fucking, he ordered me to stand up and bend my ass over on the edge of the couch. Quickly obliging, I got on the edge of the couch, with one leg lifted on it and my ass in the air, waiting. I almost lost my damn mind when I felt Ronnie enter me from the back.

We fucked for the next twenty minutes or so, with both of us trying our best to contain our sounds. When we were done, I went to the hall bathroom to clean myself up. I grabbed a washrag out of the closet in the bathroom and wet it with hot water. Sitting on the toilet, I washed my pussy and smiled at the fact that we didn't use a condom, and this time, Ronnie had to know what he was doing.

Lord knows I didn't want any more kids; hell, I was barely there for the ones I had now, but having Ronnie's baby would be a goldmine. After I was done washing up, I came out of the bathroom as Ronnie was coming down the stairs, fully dressed.

We locked eyes, but he looked away and went back into the living room.

"Well, I guess this is my cue to leave." I announced as I went back over to the couch where he was sitting.

"I'll call you later." he said, not even looking up in my direction.

"Okay, cool." I grabbed my purse and left out.

I got inside my car and drove off, smiling. I'm sure Ronnie's sudden attitude change had something to do with the fact that we just fucked unprotected. Oh well, he better suck that shit up because if I was pregnant, there was no way in hell I was getting rid of this meal ticket.

Chapter Thirty-Three

KIM

Laying in my bed asleep, I woke up to banging on my front door. I looked over at the clock on the nightstand and saw that it was seven in the fucking morning. Still hearing the banging on my front door, I sucked my teeth as I snatched the covers off me and went into the living room to see who the hell was banging on my shit like they were crazy. Looking through the peephole, I saw Nick standing outside my door.

I debated on if I should open it or not, but I knew that if I didn't, his ass would just continue to stand out there and knock.

"It's too early for this shit, Nick." I said, snatching the door open with an attitude.

"You think I give a fuck about what time it is?" he yelled as he pushed past me and walked inside.

I closed the door and turned around to see what it was that he wanted. I already knew he was probably about to question me about seeing his bitch at the mall yesterday. I admit, seeing her there with Sky was surprising. I had no idea that those two knew one another. Both of those bitches were looking at me with their noses in the air, which caused me to laugh as I passed them.

I know Sky, and knew that she probably wanted to beat my ass, and secretly, she could. Sky was a beast with her hands, and even though I was all talk and no bite, I still wouldn't show fear to her ass.

"I thought I made shit clear to yo' ass earlier when I said that I didn't do drama." He stood there looking at me, talking as if I was a fucking child.

"What the fuck are you talking about?"

I may have seen his hoe at the mall, but I didn't say shit to her ass.

"I already heard about what happened yesterday, but what I didn't know, was that you watched that fuck nigga rape Sky." He blurted out.

Oh shit! I didn't expect for that to come out of Nick's mouth. Panic started to set in. The only people that knew about that was me and Sky. I guess the hoe must have run her mouth to Nick's chick, but if Nick knew about it, then that means Ronnie would know also. It was bad enough his ass was already crazy, but when it came to Sky, Ronnie could lose his mind.

Shit, the streets were already saying how he was the one responsible for doing Gerald's ass in.

"Whoever told you that shit is a fucking lie. I never watched Gerald rape Sky." I lied.

Next thing I knew, Nick rushed over to me and threw me up against the wall with his hand wrapped around my neck.

"How the fuck you know I was talking about Gerald when I didn't say a name, bitch!" He squeezed my neck tight.

I tried to remove his hands, but he wasn't budging.

"The baby." I struggled to say.

Nick must have understood me because he let me go. I slid down the wall, coughing, trying to catch my breath. Suddenly, I was being pulled up by my hair, which caused me to scream out in pain.

"I don't know what type of games you fucking playing, but I'm the wrong one to be playing them with. Bitch, from here on out, the only time I better hear from yo' ass is when you have that baby so I can get my DNA test. If the baby turns out to be mine, I'm taking my daughter from yo' hoe ass. What type of female stands by and watches a coward mutha-fucka rape another woman?" Nick screamed in my face with spit hitting me at the same time.

He snatched his hand away from the grip on my hair and pushed me to the side. Looking at me one last time, Nick walked out of my front door, slamming it. I knew that I fucked up big time now, but I wasn't about to sit back and let Nick think he could treat me like shit. I was about to make this nigga's life a living fucking hell!

Using the wall to help me up off the floor, I walked back into my bedroom. I looked into the mirror on my dresser and saw that my hair was a mess from his ass pulling it. Cutting my eyes over to the perfume bottle sitting on the side, I picked it up, closed my eyes, and hit myself hard across the face with it.

"Ah!" I screamed out in pain.

Opening my eyes, I saw that the right side of my face was already swelling and bruised. I then walked over to the closet door and smashed my left arm in it hard, screaming out in pain from that also. Hearing a cracking sound, I knew that I broke something. Pain was an understatement for what I was in. Breathing heavy, I walked over to my nightstand and grabbed my cell phone. I dialed 911, preparing myself to put on the best damn show!

"Nine-one-one, what's your emergency?" the operator said into the phone.

"I need the police to come over to my place. My baby daddy just beat me up and left." I cried into the phone.

I gave her the address and she assured me that someone was on the way. Hanging up the phone, I smiled as I walked back out to the living room. With my right arm, I started throwing shit around and breaking the mirror and vase I had in the living room. I needed to make it look like Nick's ass was trying to fuck me up. The pain from my face and left arm were hurting like hell, but this wasn't shit compared to what Nick's ass was about to feel.

Chapter Thirty-Four

NICK

I was sitting at my desk in my home office that I converted one of the extra bedrooms into, in deep thought. Although my cousin, Sheila, the one who was going to run my upcoming daycare center, had just called me and said that we got the grant that would allow low-income families to use their voucher for their kids to attend my daycare, I was still in a fucked up mood.

I just couldn't believe this shit I got myself into. For the longest, I had always made conscience decisions on everything I did. From running with Ronnie selling dope, making my money, up to the bitches I fucked with. When I got with Katrice, I just knew everything was complete. I got out of the game and she was about to have my first born; a son.

I also had more than enough money and invested it wisely

so that if I chose not to, I wouldn't have to lift another finger in my life. I was a prime example of a dude who had it all and still wasn't satisfied. There was no reason why I fucked around on Katrice with Kim. I honestly just did the shit because I could.

A lot of times, a man doesn't need a reason to cheat. You can have the best woman in the world and still fuck shit up. I never in my life begged any woman to not leave me, but when Katrice was telling me how she was leaving and moving out, I felt like I couldn't breathe. Some would probably call me a pussy, but I didn't give a damn.

I was willing to do whatever it took to make sure Katrice stayed in my life, so if I had to beg, then so be it. Getting pussy that day was a bonus, but now she was back to walking around the house, ignoring me. Her baby shower was scheduled for this weekend, and instead of her being excited like any first-time mother should, she wasn't. The only reason she was having it was because of Sky.

Truthfully, my son didn't need shit because I made sure of that. He already had two rooms because everything couldn't fit in his nursery. So, since Sky was the one in charge of the baby shower, I knew what was going on with the planning. I made sure to pay for everything pertaining to it as well. I told Sky that there was no limit on what Katrice could have. So, as any woman would do without a budget, Sky went all out.

The shower was being held at Sky and Ronnie's place, where she had the ice sculptures, a professional decorator, photo booth, all types of games, DJ, and even some adult themed goody bags she had full of freaky shit. Not to mention, all the food that she and Ms. Mary would be cooking. I suggested to just have it catered, but Ms. Mary wasn't having that shit.

All in all, I knew that Katrice would enjoy the baby shower, and it would be good to see a smile on my baby's face, knowing that I put it there. Hopefully, it would also take my mind off everything that had been going on. Besides my personal life, I learned that we also had someone out there who was watching Ronnie and me. The surprising part was that it was a female.

Right now, we both needed to have our feet on the pavement and ears to the streets, trying to find out who the fuck was trying to get us, but instead, we were too busy trying to fix our households. Ronnie had been laying low, chilling lately. He and Sky were still living separately and I could tell it was fucking with him. He and I never spoke about our situations, but we knew what time it was.

Lost in my thoughts, I didn't hear Katrice when she came into the office.

"Nick, there are two police officers at the door asking for you." Katrice stood in the doorway, looking panicked.

One thing I didn't deal with was the fucking pigs, so there shouldn't be a reason why they were at my fucking house.

"Fuck they want?" I asked her, standing up.

"I don't know, they just asked for you." She answered.

I left out of the office with Katrice trailing behind me

down the stairs. I saw two white ass cops standing at my front door entrance, looking around.

"Can I help you?" I asked them as I stood in front of them.

"Yes, are you Nicholas Brown?" the pale, fat ass one asked me.

"Yeah, what's up?"

"Sir, you are under arrest for the assault of a Ms. Kimberly Ryan."

The other officer spoke as he came closer to me with his handcuffs out.

"What the fuck you talking about? Who the hell is Kimberly Ryan?" Katrice yelled out from behind me.

"Ma'am, we're going to need you to back up." the officer who had just put me in cuffs said to her.

"Aye man, you came here for me, not her, so address all your comments to me. Katrice, call Ronnie and tell him what's going down. He'll know what to do; I'll be back." I smirked, looking at the cop.

Katrice nodded her head up and down, crying, giving me confirmation that she was about to do what I had just asked her.

"You have the right to remain silent..." the officer began to read me my rights.

I tuned his ass out as they both walked me to their squad car and put me in the back. This was the first time that I had ever been arrested. I knew who Kimberly Ryan was when they said the hoe's name. I've been doing dirt in the streets for years and never got caught up with any damn police, yet, they come to my house on some bullshit ass charge, talking about an assault on Kim's stupid ass. I promise you, baby or not, that hoe better hide under a rock from here on out because her ass is just as good as dead.

Chapter Thirty-Five

RONNIE

I was in my car, leaving my lawyer's office after dropping off Nick's bail money. He hadn't been to court yet, but he was scheduled to go in the morning. I'm sure his ass would get a bond due to him not having a prior record, but you never know how this shit would play out with this crooked ass system. When I got the call earlier from Katrice, crying, telling me that the police had just left her and Nick's place and that they had arrested him, my mind instantly went to Gerald.

My initial thought was that they found out we killed his ass, but when she told me that they arrested him on assault charges for a bitch named Kimberly Ryan, I sighed in relief. Yeah, he was in jail, but this shit was peanuts compared to what he could be sitting for. This is why I tried to warn Nick about that hoe Kim in the beginning. Her ass was capable of underhanded shit, and now my boy was caught up in her web again.

But right now, I was in no position to dissect Nick's situation. My shit was so fucked up and to make matters worse, I slipped up and fucked Ebony's ass without a rubber. Hell, I don't even know if this was the first time we fucked without one, but I do know this was the first time I was in a clear state of mind, so I should have known better.

Ebony was cool peoples to have around to fuck from time to time, but she wasn't Sky. My head was so gone thinking about Sky and missing her that I was out here being reckless. I know one thing, though, if Ebony's ass was pregnant, she was getting an abortion, voluntarily or involuntarily. Sky was the only woman walking around here with my child, and whether we get back together or not, she'll still be the only woman that I choose to have my baby.

I was heading to the club now to pick Ebony up so that I could go with her to her doctor's appointment to see if her ass was pregnant. She insisted that I meet her there since she was at the club, working at the bar for the afternoon shift, filling in for one of the bartenders, but I told her ass that I would pick her up and we'd go together. I needed to make sure that I was there myself to find out what was going on.

That night after she left my house, it took me a week to call her. That's when I told her that I thought she should go to the doctor to see if she was pregnant. Her ass agreed to do so with so much enthusiasm in her voice that I took the phone away from my ear and looked at that shit as if I could see her. Pulling up into the club's parking lot, I sent her a text, letting her know I was outside.

She replied, telling me she was coming out. A couple of seconds later, Ebony came walking to my car in a pair of high-waisted booty shorts that had her ass cheeks hanging out, a cutoff shirt with her damn nipples showing, and a pair of diamond studded sandals. I ain't gone lie, she looked sexy as fuck, but who the fuck would go to a doctor's appointment dressed like this?

Getting inside the car, I pulled off before she even had the chance to buckle her seat belt.

"Well, hello to you too." She spoke first in a sarcastic tone.

"You couldn't change into something more decent than that?" I asked her, bypassing that speaking shit.

"I could, but I chose not to." she replied, getting slick.

Already I was getting irritated with her and her slick ass mouth. I hope she didn't think I was questioning her about her clothes because I was jealous or some other shit like that; that was far from the case. I was the one that was about to be seen with her ass in public, and I didn't want the unnecessary attention. The rest of the drive was quiet with Ebony on her phone, looking at some dumb ass videos and laughing; shit sounded like some loud ass bitches fighting.

I shook my head as I headed to the Biscayne Area where her appointment was. I prayed like hell this chick wasn't pregnant, because after today, I wasn't fucking with her ass anymore. Just as expected in this area, we were backed up in traffic and were at a standstill. Since we weren't moving, I pulled my phone out to see if I had any text messages, only to see that Sky had sent me a text.

I opened it up, expecting to see her telling me something about Imani, but instead, she sent me a message telling me that she missed me. A smile spread so wide across my face. This was the first time Sky had told me anything like this in a long time, and I missed that shit.

Right when I was about to reply, I heard a loud crash from behind me. Turning around, I saw a white van make its way through the other cars, hitting them, not giving a fuck as it pulled up next to the passenger side of my car. Before I could react, the van doors opened and started shooting at my car. I heard Ebony scream as I grabbed her and yanked her down on the seat.

My gun was in my waistband, so I pulled it out and started shooting blindly out the passenger window where the van was, while I laid down in the driver's seat. I knew that I had been shot because I started feeling a burning sensation going through my body. Next thing I knew, the gunfire stopped. I lifted my head up slightly to peek out and see what was going on, when I heard someone approach my side of the car.

I looked over in that direction instead and saw that it was the same bitch who Rob showed me in the pictures.

"This is for my husband, Damon!" She aimed her gun at my face and pulled the trigger.

I fell back on my seat and my eyes started to feel heavy. The only thing I could think about was Sky and Imani. I tried to move, but my whole body felt like it was stuck in cement. Not able to fight it anymore, I closed my eyes and welcomed the darkness.

Chapter Thirty-Six

SKY

*E*very time you think things couldn't get any worse, they always do. Katrice had been to my house, crying her eyes out since Nick had been arrested. When she told me how they came to their house to get him, and the female's name who he supposedly assaulted, I couldn't believe that shit. When I told her that the female was Kim, that didn't make things better. She went from crying to cursing Nick's ass out all in one breath as if he was standing in her face.

I could understand, though. Shit, had it been me, I think my ass would be in jail right now for killing Ronnie's ass. Speaking of which, I still hated the way things were between us. When he dropped Imani back off home from spending the weekend with him, he handed her off to Ms. Mary and didn't say shit to me.

Hearing the things and heartache that Katrice was going through started to make me look at things for what they were with Ronnie and me. In all fairness, I never had to deal with Ronnie and him cheating on me with other females. He was right, though; all he ever did was love me and be there for me, and I've just been pushing him away. The only reason I asked for space in the first place was because I feared he would get tired of always having to be there for me.

It had nothing to do with him at all, and it was time that I let him know the truth and get my man back. Sitting on the couch, I picked my phone up and sent him a text telling him that I missed him, and put it back down. I became nervous waiting on his reply. I prayed that it wasn't too late and that he felt the same way.

"Have you heard from Ronnie? Did he mention anything about what's going on with Nick?" Katrice asked me.

"No, but I did just send him a text telling him that I missed him." I confessed to her.

"Girl, I knew it! Your ass couldn't keep holding out on that man for too long. Honestly, Ronnie is a good dude. You don't have to worry about him out here getting stripper bitches pregnant and then going to jail behind them."

"Nick is a good dude too; his ass is just stupid. Trust me, I'm sure he learned his lesson." I tried comforting her.

I didn't want Katrice stressing more than she already was with my nephew in her stomach.

"Um-huh, time will tell. Can you please just call Ronnie and ask him about Nick for me, please?"

I reluctantly picked my phone back up and dialed his number. I was so nervous that you would think this would be my first time talking to him. The phone rang four times before a female's voice answered it.

"Uh, hello?" I said, confused, sitting up on the couch.

I know damn well this nigga didn't have another bitch answering his fucking phone!

"Hi, are you looking for Ronald Johnson?" the lady asked me.

"Yes, I am. Who are you?"

"I'm a nurse here at Jackson Memorial Hospital. Mr. Johnson was rushed here to the trauma center with multiple gunshot wounds. We were just about to contact next of kin when you called."

All I heard was gunshot wounds and Jackson Memorial Hospital.

"Oh my God, I'm on my way!" I shouted and jumped up from the couch.

"Sky, what happened?" Katrice asked.

"Ronnie's been shot and is at Jackson Hospital; I gotta get there!" I said in a panic as I ran up the stairs to Ms. Mary's room.

I opened her door to find her sitting on the edge of her bed with a sleeping Imani laying in her lap, as she was braiding her hair.

"Ms. Mary, Ronnie is in the hospital; he's been shot!" I cried out.

"Oh, Lord! Is he alright?" she asked as she placed Imani on the bed and walked over to me.

"I'm not sure, but I'm on my way there now." I informed her.

"Okay, you go ahead. I'll wake Imani up and be there shortly. Don't worry, God ain't ready for him yet."

I rushed back down the stairs and Katrice offered to drive since I wasn't in the right frame of mind. On the ride over to the hospital, so many thoughts were going through my mind. What if he died and I never got the chance to tell him how sorry I was for the way I had been acting? I was in such a daze that I didn't even notice that we were already there until Katrice told me.

Getting out of the car, we rushed inside to the nurse's station and asked the nurse that was sitting there for information on Ronnie.

"I'll notify the doctor that you're here, and he'll be out to talk to you." the nurse told me.

I stood to the side, crying with Katrice close by, hugging me. I honestly didn't know what I was going to do if Ronnie was dead. Finally, a doctor came out and asked for the family of Ronald Johnson.

"That's us." I said in a rush as I damn near ran up to him.

"Hi, I'm Dr. Glover. I've been treating Mr. Johnson since he was brought in. He's been shot five times; once in the left leg, once in the shoulder, twice in the upper torso and once in the face." he went on to explain.

"Oh my God, he's dead!" I cried out.

Katrice grabbed me tightly and kept me from falling to the floor.

"As of now, he's not. He's holding on, so it's a touch and go situation. We just finished surgery on him where we removed all the bullets, but had to leave the fragments of the one in his face. His jaw is wired shut. Had he not been shot at close range in the face, I'm sure he wouldn't have made it; right now, he's stable, but he did slip into a coma after surgery. The passenger of the vehicle was also a lucky young lady as well." Dr. Glover added.

I looked up at his last comment.

"Passenger?" I said, confused.

"Yes, a young lady was brought in with him. She was shot also and lost a lot of blood, but we were able to stop the bleeding and gave her a successful transfusion, which also saved her baby.

Baby? I looked over at Katrice, who more than likely was thinking the same thing I was. Just like that, my tears ceased. I know damn well this muthafucka wasn't laid up in this hospital with holes all in his ass, with some bitch lying next to him, and she was pregnant! I knew that if I acted a fool and continued to act clueless as to who this other female was, the doctor would catch on and not let me see Ronnie or her, so I turned on my street smarts.

"Oh, that must have been my cousin Shonda that was with Ronnie. Can I please see them both, Doctor? Our other family is on their way and I want to be able to tell them that I saw them both and that they will be okay." I lied my ass off.

I even turned my tears back on to lay it on thick.

"Okay, but only for a quick minute. They are both in ICU and are heavily sedated. Follow me." He said to us.

Katrice and I walked behind the doctor as he took us on the ICU floor.

"Can I see my female cousin first, please?" I asked.

"Sure, she's in this room. Once you're done, have the nurse take you to see Mr. Johnson. If you have any questions, make sure you have them look for me." Dr. Glover gave me a soft pat on my back and walked away.

I stood outside of the door of the woman who was with Ronnie at the time he got shot. I didn't know what the fuck I was about to walk in on, but I needed to know what the fuck was going on. Katrice grabbed hold of my hand because she saw how hesitant I was.

"I'm right here, bestie" she assured me.

We both walked in the first room, and sure enough, there was a female lying in bed, hooked up to tubes, and she appeared to be asleep. As I walked closer to the bed to get a better look at her, I stopped dead in my tracks. I just knew my eyes were playing fucking tricks on me.

"You okay, Sky? Do you know her?" Katrice questioned as I stood there, stone still.

I couldn't believe the shit I was seeing.

"Uh, yes, I do." I stammered. "That's my sister, Isis."

"Sister? What the fuck was she doing with—" Katrice stopped midway into her sentence as if she just answered her own question.

I was still standing there, staring at Isis laying there, trying to wrap my mind around the fact that my own sister and Ronnie were dealing with one another. Then suddenly, I remembered the doctor saying that her baby survived! I turned around and went out to the nurse's station that was in front of Isis' room.

"Can you tell me what room Ronald Johnson is in? I asked her.

She gave me the room number, which was two doors down from Isis, and I marched my ass right in there. When I got inside, Ronnie was also laying in the bed, but he was hooked up to more machines than Isis was and his leg was up in the air in a sling. I should be crying, begging him to make it so that he could come back home to Imani and me, but instead, I walked over to the bed and bent down to his ear.

"I'm not sure if you can hear me or not, but if you're not already dead, muthafucka I hope you rot in hell. You and yo' bitch, Isis." I whispered in a low, menacing tone.

It was as if Ronnie heard me because the machines suddenly started going off. The nurses heard them and rushed into the room.

"Code blue! Get the doctor in here, he's crashing!" one nurse yelled.

I stood back in the corner of the room and watched as the doctor and nurses worked on Ronnie.

"I need the crash cart, we're losing him!" the doctor yelled.

Everyone was moving around so fast in the room, trying to save Ronnie's life, while I just stood there, emotionless.

"Ma'am, we need you to clear the room." One of the nurses said to me.

Not protesting, I walked out of the room, not even looking back.

"Let's go, Katrice. I need to get back home to my baby." I calmly said as I started walking towards the exit to leave the floor.

"But, Sky, Ronnie is in there dying; you can't just leave!" Katrice cried out.

"Watch me! That nigga had the nerve to be fucking my own damn sister and the bitch is pregnant! You think I'm supposed to feel some type of sympathy for him and that bitch! I'm done with all this shit! Fuck Ronnie and fuck Isis!" I screamed out as I turned around and left.

From here on out, I didn't give a damn if Ronnie or Isis' ass flat lined; I was done playing the fool. The old Sky is back...

Made in the USA
Monee, IL
11 February 2020